DIAMONDS IN THE DUST

by

SHIRLEY MOWAT TUCKER

ATHANATOS
PUBLISHING GROUP

DIAMONDS
IN THE
DUST

by

SHIRLEY MOWAT TUCKER

ATHANATOS
PUBLISHING GROUP

Diamonds in the Dust
By Shirley Mowat Tucker

Website: www.diamondsinthedust.net

Winner of Athanatos Christian Ministry's 2011 Christian Novel Contest: http://www.christianwritingcontest.com

Published by Athanatos Publishing Group

ISBN 978-0-9822776-9-0

Cover by Julius Broqueza

For Monty Sholund who said I could, and I believed him.

Acknowledgements

Writing a book is more about teamwork than I ever imagined. Alongside me a disparate band of people dipped into my life to encourage, edit, give feedback, keep me from making stupid mistakes which all added to my knowledge and helped refine the finished product.

So I need to say thank you to:

Anthony Horvath, of Athanatos Christian Ministries, for making a dream become a reality and doing it with such openhearted generosity and patience,

to my wonderful Mark for clearing the runway so I could fly and for still loving and believing in me 33 years later,

to my kids Dusty and Jenn, Cathy-Jo and Dan; Why am I so special to have you?

to Mom, 93, and still loving, still forgiving, still my hero; to Dad, gone but not without first nurturing in my heart a love of story–a true gentleman,

to all my dear family and friends: Linda Lagerwey and the Tuesday ladies group–troupers, warriors and encouragers; Elaine Phillips, Sue Lankers, Sue Williams, Lynn Hodge and Richard Rufus-Ellis for editing at different stages,

to Busisiwe Marule for checking the siSwati/Zulu and to Ian Milne for letting me bend his ear about zoological issues,

to Mary Rosenblum, from Long Ridge Writers Group, who inspired me to keep going.

to God, who, because he isn't here physically, chooses you and me to touch the hurting, the damaged and the hungry.

CHAPTER 1

She'd got away. The man slowed down to a jog and took a deep breath to quiet the hammering in his head and ease the pain in his lungs. He looked up in time to catch one last glimpse of her before she disappeared around the bend. He'd never catch her now. "I'll get you, you worthless dung beetle. Next time."

After all that planning she'd slipped through his fingers. He kicked at a large, black rhino beetle struggling through the rain-muddied path in front of him and watched it tumble into the churning waters of the river two meters to his left. Going after her during the day had been a big mistake. Now there were witnesses.

He'd take a short cut and met the others back at the car. The short cut proved to be a long cut as the sodden earth sucked at his shoes like quick-sand and slowed him down to a crawl. But it was way too risky going back the way he'd come.

By the time he reached his car, hidden in some brush, he could feel the weight of his blunder lighten. She'd be back. She'd never leave the others.

*

It wasn't the lightning that frightened Ida Morgan. She stopped munching on her toast to listen. Thunder grumbled in bad-temper then suddenly threw its venom at the earth, striking its target in a blinding bolt of light. This was a big one. She covered her ears and waited. A deafening crack–splintering and rumbling slowly into silence.

It was what followed that alarmed her. A thin wailing sound slashed at the air for several seconds then that, too, subsided. Someone was in trouble out there but the last time she'd gone to help a person, Tony had died.

Ida jumped up, threw the last morsel of honey toast onto the side-plate and dashed over to the lounge window. At first, distinguishing anything through the driving rain was like trying to see through a striped frosted window. As the storm lessened she began to grasp the extent of the damage to her garden; ripped off branches and twigs hurled to far corners; her bougainvilleas and roses stripped and their bruised flowers strewn across patches of lawn which stood like miniature islands in a flood plain. But no sign of life.

Beyond her fenced garden she noticed the once towering wild fig tree had taken the fury of the lightning strike. Neatly carved down the middle, half the tree had collapsed sideways over the swollen stream whose rushing waters tumbled under it. From where she stood, it looked as though the tips of its branches reached the bank on the far side. This side of the stricken tree remained standing but listed to the right. No sign of movement out there either.

Within minutes the gurgle of rainwater down the drainpipe slowed to a trickle. The storm ended as it often did in the lowveld of South Africa, as suddenly as it had started. Ida hesitated at her front door, clutching the lower gate key. She looked down at her soil-stained 'takkies' and wondered how well they'd keep the water out. But she knew she was just buying time. Who cared if her feet got wet? She couldn't ignore what she had heard.

She arrived at the new six foot tall wire mesh gate and stopped. Her confidence sagged. She reminded herself it wasn't so bad in the daylight when she could at least see around her and feel like she had a fighting chance. The fact it was unlikely to happen again was little comfort. With a thorough scan of the whole area she slipped the key into the lock.

Once through the gate, Ida picked her way over slippery boulders and patches of sodden grass to the stream's edge. Watchful and listening for any sign of movement, she began to question the sound she'd heard after the strike. She felt some of the tension leave her and became aware of the devastation before her. What a mess. This was going to take some cleaning up. Empty milk bottles, cool-drink containers, pieces of ragged white plastic littered the high water mark where grass and weeds lay leveled against the ground, stretching out in the direction of the water's flow.

As she rounded a rock that rose above her shoulders, a large, blue, plastic bin caught her eye. Wedged in the sheltered recess of a rock and bobbing gently some 20 feet away from her, the blue bin floated in a tangle of uprooted plants and other rubbish. The bin, though scarred by years of rough handling, was sturdy–perfect for carting litter away. If she stood on that rock over there she might be able to pull it in.

She searched around for a stick strong enough to do the job. Glancing back at the bin to gauge how long it needed to be, she grew

2

rigid. The bin began to bounce erratically from side to side as eight little black fingers emerged, gripping the lip of the container. Then faint bursts of sobbing as the fingers disappeared and the bin settled once more.

Ida sprang onto a rock to peer into the bin. A child, barely covered by the wet rags clinging to his body, faced downward, his arms and legs jammed against the corners of the bin.

"*Bambelela, ngizokusiza.* Hold on. I'll help you," Ida said in Zulu, grateful for her childhood relationships on the farm in KwaZulu-Natal. She leapt off the rock. A cursory glance around the area revealed no stick long enough to pull the bin in. She headed home, returning a few minutes later with a garden rake. Clasping her hands around the end of the rake handle she extended it over the water. It was just too short. Maybe there was extra reach using one hand while stretching out and balancing with the other.

The end of the stout wooden rake sagged but she hefted it upward and let it fall. It missed and crashed into the water. She almost had it. The second attempt snagged the bin. A startled yelp came from inside as the rake whacked the edge and sent the bin dipping and diving.

"*Kulungile.* I have you." Ida tugged at the container, feeling the resistance of clogging debris. Finally the bin broke free and she tugged it toward the rock she stood on. She knelt down next to the container. Steadying the bin with one hand, she reached out to the child with the other. "Give me your hand." The child remained glued to the bottom of the container.

Ida sank down on the rock and stretched out her legs. She hooked a toe under the edge of the rim and the bin stabilized. "What is your name?" She leaned back for a few seconds to relieve tense muscles in her neck. There was no answer but a little black face, tear tracked and taut, turned up to stare at her. Ida smiled. "I do not bite." Again she reached out her hand.

Eyes fixed on the bottom of the bin, the child slowly released pressure on the sides and suddenly grabbed Ida's hands.

Tears stung Ida's eyes. His hands were like stripped chicken bones taken from the fridge and his young body rattled with tremors. She stole a glance at him from the corner of her eye. He was taller than she had thought. Maybe eight or nine years old.

"How on earth did you end up in that bin in the middle of the storm?" Ida rubbed his bone-lumpy back while she led him along the path to the house. His only response was a frenetic clicking of teeth.

Once inside the house, she cocooned him in her bright red knitted blanket and settled him on the sofa. After starting a hot bath, she made and handed him a peanut-butter sandwich and milk. The child fought his way out of the blanket and took the plate but turned his face away. Ida strode over to the old Steinway upright, stretched out nimble fingers, and began to coax out the rhythmic sounds of Black Gospel in "Oh, happy day." Every now and then she raised her eyes to study the child through the mirror above the piano.

Torn between the music and the food he finally decided he could have both. He attacked the food, his chin jutting out from side to side in time to the beat of the music. He stuffed in the food until his bulging cheeks made it difficult to draw his lips together. No problem. He chewed anyway, swallowing hunks of bread, and in no time he was done, sending the last few bites down with the milk. Little fingers chased crumbs around the plate and by the time he'd finished, his shivering had stopped, too.

Ida ended the song and plopped down next to him on the sofa. "What is your name?"

The child looked down.

"Is it Vusi?" A shake of the head.

"Phineas?" He frowned.

"Okay," she said, straightening up. "It's Moses then." Ida pulled him up. "Time for a nice warm bath, Moses."

Moses' face remained blank. Ida made washing body movements. A tiny light flickered in the brown eyes. Ah!

Closing the bathroom door on the child she went in search of a T-shirt and a pair of shorts from a time long before she'd reached her present five feet one inch. When she returned with them she stopped short. Moses stood in the middle of the bath, fully clothed, scrubbing both the clothes and himself with energy. Brown water slopped up the side of the bath leaving a line of scum in its wake.

"Moses."

The child stopped abruptly and stared at the wall.

"Sorry," Ida said, turning her eyes away from him. "It is easier to wash yourself when you take your clothes off first. You can dry

4

yourself with this towel. Then put these clothes on." She looped them over the rail. "They are too big but they're clean." She began to help pull off sopping rags, wandering what color they used to be. Then she looked down. Her head snapped up.

"You're not Moses. You're Mosesina." She stared into the face of the girl. She paused. "What the heck," she said. "Moses is easier."

While she waited, Ida picked up the phone and dialed White River Police Station. "I'd like to report a missing child," she said. "Actually, she's not missing; I found her." A pause. "I don't know. She can't speak. No, she's not dead. She's just too traumatized to speak. Maybe you can get her to talk?" She gave her address, "It's 6 Jacaranda Drive." She concluded the call and waited for the police to arrive.

On her way to see how Moses was doing, she heard the phone. "No, Mr. Mbuso," Ida said into the phone, clutching it tightly. "I know how important it is. I'll have it done in time. By Wednesday next week. I promise." She caught her breath and continued. "Yes, first thing." She slowly returned the phone. Another weekend spent working. She couldn't lose this job. If her finances didn't improve soon she'd be losing her home. Things had been very tight since Tony had gone.

When Moses still had not returned from the bathroom, Ida went to investigate. She heard sounds of movement behind the door. On opening it, she saw Moses on the floor mopping up the last splash of water. The child had almost done a better job of the bathroom than she would have. Moses flipped the towel onto the side of the bath and smiled from behind her hand.

"*Ngiyabonga*, Moses. Thank you."

The bell at the front gate rang at five minutes before eight. Moses swung round to face Ida at the kitchen table and started to rise. Ida caught her by the arm. "It's okay, Moses. I think it's the police. They have come to help you." She stepped over to the intercom at the kitchen door while checking through the kitchen window. A police GTI was parked outside her gate. She pressed the gate buzzer.

The sergeant hoisted himself out of the car. He sauntered to the gate, leaning backward somewhat, in order to carry the load of his ample stomach in front of him. Behind him, an officer, whose immaculate uniform ended at his mirror-clean boots, both minus

5

shoelaces.

"Mrs. Morgan?"

"Good morning." She took the sergeant's hand. "Thank you for coming."

"I am Sergeant Jawena." He faced the other man. "This is Officer Dube." Officer Dube's eyes were active in his still face, taking in the house, the garden, the car and finally settling on Ida. He investigated her, too, but did not attempt to greet her. Ida wondered if the small patch of white hair at his right temple was the result of the parasite Bilharzia or if that was an old wives' tale.

"Tell me what happened here," Sergeant Jawena said, his round face serious and attentive.

As Ida explained, she looked back at the house. The tip of Moses' head showed above the lace curtains in the kitchen, then disappeared.

When she had finished, Sergeant Jawena shuffled his feet on the driveway and said nothing for several seconds.

"You can help her?" Ida asked.

"Mrs. Morgan, we can help this girl." He shook his head slowly. "But it is a big problem. Everyday we are hearing about children who are needing help. It will take some time."

"All she needs is someone to find out who she is and where she lives." Officer Dube took a sudden interest. "They are too many," he said. His restless eyes were off again, searching.

"Too many problems or too many children?" The tension in Ida's neck was returning. "Why don't I get her? Maybe she'll talk to you." Ida strode over to the kitchen door and leaned through it. "Moses. Come. The policeman wants to talk to you." She tapped the side of the doorway, waiting.

"Moses?"

She looked at her watch. Time for working was being eaten up. There was no response. She stepped through the doorway. A quick search of the house revealed the front door was unlocked and the child had gone.

She hurried around the flower beds, up the garden path, and along the side of the house. No Moses. When she returned to the sergeant he was scribbling in a small notebook with a stub of pencil. Officer Dube stood peering over his shoulder. They looked up as she approached.

6

"She's gone. I've looked everywhere but I can't find her." Ida felt the heat in her face.

"Maybe she has done something wrong. She does not want to be caught," Officer Dube said, eyes narrowed, as he stared at the stream beyond the front fence. Sergeant Jawena glared at him.

"Maybe she lives nearby. Maybe she has gone home." The Sergeant closed his notebook and stuffed it into his top pocket with his pudgy hands.

"Shouldn't we look for her?" Ida said.

"These children, they are clever." Officer Dube stepped up close to Ida, hunting for something in her eyes. "She will be okay."

Sergeant Jawena stepped between them. "Mrs. Morgan, I can see you are worried about her. If she comes back you can phone me and we will come to get her."

Ida ran into the house to get her diary and a pen. She wrote down Jawena's number then watched the men leave. What did the officer mean, 'these children'?

That afternoon Ida sat at her antique writing desk in her small bedroom. She wasn't into antiques. She wasn't into any particular style of furniture, come to think of it. A desk was to work on, not look at. She picked at the point of her blunt pencil and peered out the window. What happened to the child? She straightened her back, picked up a ball point pen and stared at the leather bound ledger in front of her. She shook her head and was soon lost in her bookkeeping work.

Before she knew it, the sun had disappeared behind the line of granite hills on the horizon and left a crimson bouquet in the sky. She headed to the kitchen.

She lifted an egg to crack open on the side of a stainless steel bowl when she heard it—a faint tapping at the kitchen door. She stood still and listened. There it was again. Without a sound she stepped sideways to stare out the window. The gate was still locked. She moved over to the sink, stretching herself over it and twisting her body so she could see who was standing at the door.

"Who is it?" No one answered. "Go away or I'll phone the police," she called out. At that there was a flash of movement from behind the door and a child streaked across Ida's vision, heading toward the gate.

Ida flew over to the door, unlocking it. "Moses," she shouted. "*Kulungile*. Come back. I thought you were a *tsotsi*." The child stopped and glanced behind her. Ida caught up with her and placed an arm around the thin shoulders. "Come inside. You can sleep here tonight."

Moses stood inside the kitchen door with her arms linked behind her back, waiting. At first Ida did not notice. Then…

"Oh. You can sit down." Ida indicated a chair at the table.

She searched around in her rather limited Zulu vocabulary for the word "bacon". "Tonight we will eat pig and egg," she said instead. She'd been keeping the bacon for a special occasion and this was it. The aroma of sizzling bacon drew attention to her hunger. "I could eat a whole pig tonight." For the first time, Moses' mouth stretched in a smile.

Together they sat at opposite ends of the small round kitchen table, eating, and sipping hot sweet tea. Ida tried to make conversation.

"I feel like I'm talking into a phone with no one at the other end," Ida said, observing Moses eat small bites of food using the tips of her thin fingers. "I see pig is not your first choice in dinner," she said in English. Moses stared back for a moment then went back to her food.

Ida wiped the crumbs off the side of her mouth and she scraped back her chair. Leaning over the table to gather the dirty dishes she said, "I have work to do. Come, I will show you where you can sleep."

Moses followed Ida into a small room where the single bed, spread with a multi-colored crocheted quilt, was already made up. She switched on the light and took Moses' hand, leading her to the side table. "You switch the lamp on here." She showed her.

Moses let go of her hand and walked around the bed taking in the room. When her feet touched the soft rug at her feet she bent down and her young fingers caressed it. Then, lowering herself onto it, she lay down with her legs tucked up to her chin. With her cheek she stroked its thick softness.

Ida hurried out before the waterworks started. No more tears. Losing your husband to murder at 40 taught you tears don't change anything. She gave her head a quick shake and moved off to her desk.

Shortly after Ida had settled back to her work she heard the *ffssh* of a tap running and the clatter of dishes from the kitchen. She pushed back her chair and went to check. Moses stood on the stool next to the kitchen sink washing the supper dishes. Just louder than her breath came a whispered tune. Ida grinned. So the vocal chords were in working order. She walked up behind the child and raised her arms to place them around the slim body but memories of the past pulled them down again to her sides. Silently she stepped out of the room.

The cat. She'd almost forgotten. She moved over to the pantry and retrieved the cat food. But when she picked up the cat's bowl she saw the food had not been touched. She opened the back door and called into the night. "Cricket?" The cat with only three more lives left did not respond. Maybe his nose was out of joint with having an unfamiliar guest here. She closed the door and headed to her office. Picking up her pen, she settled down to her bookkeeping.

By twelve o'clock that night Ida was nodding off at her desk. After her five-thirty start this morning she was finished. She went through to the lounge and sank into the cool leather of her favorite arm chair. Her eyes closed. For the first time in two years she was glad she had lived today. But if she sat here any longer she wouldn't have the energy to go to bed.

She sighed, planted her feet together in front of her and pushed herself out the armchair. After placing the tufted seat pillow in the center of the chair-back to cover the worn patch where she'd been sitting, she made her way down the short, tiled passage to the spare bedroom. She stood for a moment with her ear against the door then silently opened it.

The lace curtain at the window swelled gently as a cool breeze blew through the open but barred window. Moonlight streamed onto the bed. She stiffened. The bed was still made up and as empty as when she'd left it that morning.

"Moses?" she said softly. She waited. Her head twisted around to scan the house behind her. She took a step into the room. Listening. Only the muted sound of a dog barking and the incessant chirping of a summer cricket.

"Moses?" A few steps to the end of the bed. As she rounded the bed, her slipper connected with something hard on the floor. She jumped back, slapping her hand over her mouth, and stumbled onto the bed. In front of her, the small body of Moses shot up and staggered over to the window, falling into a tiny whimpering ball.

Ida pressed her fingers against her thumping temples. "I'm so sorry," she said. The whites of the child's eyes stared back. Ida sank onto her haunches in front of her and reached out her hands. "Beds are for sleeping on." She patted the bed. "You don't have to sleep on the floor."

She walked over to the light switch, and flicked it on. Then moving over to the bed, flung back the sheet and blanket, lay down, covered herself and pretended to snore with a loud voice and wide open mouth. She peeped through her fingers at Moses still sitting against the wall. The child's face softened but Ida noticed her repeatedly sneak a glance at the cupboard door.

Ida looked from Moses to the cupboard and back again. "What's in the cupboard?" she said. "Moses?" Her voice a harsh whisper. The child dropped her head on her knees and rocked back and forward, keening in a low voice.

Ida rose slowly, pausing each time the bed creaked. When she was upright, she tiptoed out the room and rushed to the lounge, stumbling over the edge of the grass rug, and lunged for the phone. Stabbing at the numbers with trembling fingers she began to tap out 013 750 0888 for the police. When she reached the 5 her head shot up and her fingers stopped. If the child was afraid of something in the cupboard, why had she been sleeping peacefully on the floor? Slowly she replaced the phone.

She reached into the broom cupboard and grabbed the heavy wooden handle of the broom, just in case, and crept back to the bedroom. Moses was quiet now but still sat crumpled against the wall. Her eyes widened when she saw Ida with the broom and scrambled to get on her feet.

Ida placed a finger to her mouth. "Shh." With the broom held rigid in front of her she edged toward the cupboard and extended her free hand to grasp the handle. The door burst open and the cupboard came to life with high pitched screams. A jumble of cardboard boxes and years of stored odds and ends exploded out of the cupboard.

Ida snatched up the other end of the broom, snapped it sideways in front of her body. She stepped back. The avalanche of her belongings settled and her eyes became accustomed to the shadows in the cupboard. Trying to melt into the back of the cupboard, two ragged children clung to each other.

Her head slumped forward. For a moment she stood with her eyes jammed shut. A migraine was on its way.

"How did they get in here?" she asked, flopping onto the edge of the bed.

Moses stared down at the floor.

"*Ja.* I know you can hear me," she said under her breath in English. The children in the cupboard remained very still. Only their eyes moved as they glanced back and forth from Ida to Moses. "*Wozani.* Come," Ida said quietly, bending forward then beckoning them with her fingers. In unison they glanced over at Moses who flicked her wrist and signaled them to come. They sidled over to Moses.

Both children appeared to be boys. Ida wasn't going to presume anything this time. The older appeared to be about six and the younger about three years old.

"Are they your brothers, Moses?"

She nodded.

"How did they get in?" Once more Moses hung her head and drew her brothers to her. The older boy pulled loose.

"I am Bandile." He tugged at his brother's arm. "He is Surprise. He has three years." The toddler pressed into his big sister, never taking his eyes off Ida. Bandile pointed at Moses. "She has twelve years."

Twelve? Poor nutrition or family genes had cleverly disguised the girl's age. Thankfully being mute did not run in the family. Ida reached out for a tissue on the side table and moved toward the youngest child's nose. He shrank back and buried his face between Moses and the wall. She gave up and crouched down to look into his eyes. "How did you get your name, Surprise?"

Bandile spoke up. "My mother, she did not know he is coming, so she call him Surprise."

"He's a surprise alright," she said in English.

She glanced at her watch. Only a few hours till the sun came up. "Before we go back to sleep, your brothers can have a quick bath. They can sleep at the end of your bed, Moses. We can talk in the morning."

She watched the children follow Moses to the bathroom. "And don't forget to take off their clothes. *Before* they get in," she called after them, smiling. "I'll bring some clean shirts." Their tatters would go in the rubbish tonight and she'd visit Price Mart tomorrow.

Maybe she didn't need the police's help. How difficult could it be to find the parents of three children?

CHAPTER 2

Ida woke suddenly to a door in the house bursting open and banging against the wall, followed by an explosion of laughter, then loud whispers. She eyed the large metal alarm clock next to her bed. 7:06 a.m. She'd slept in. She sank back onto her pillow and closed her eyes. As she lay there enjoying the fresh morning breeze laden with the sweet smell of oleander flowers through the window, she could almost hear Tony whistling in the kitchen making tea. Good strong tea with a touch of milk. A rattling of cups and a thump as he kicked the door open with his battered slippers. He filled the doorway, his black hair standing to attention and brushing the top of the doorframe.

"Wake up, my *suikerbossie*, sugar bush."

The picture in her mind faded. Even good memories carried a sting in the tail. She swung her legs over the side of the bed. Grabbing her pale blue dressing gown from behind the bedroom door she ambled to the spare room. She ran her fingers through her short thick hair, raising the sleeping curls to their daytime position.

What a racket. Ida peered around the children's doorway. Moses sat against the wall, pounding out a rhythm on an empty shoe box wedged between her feet. Bandile sat next to her, rubbing the spines of an old plastic comb with a knitting needle, his head and body weaving in four-time while he wailed out a repetitive melody. Surprise, bent at the waist, stomped his pint-sized bare feet in time to the impromptu band, his elbows jabbing at the ceiling while a huge grass lampshade on his head bounced rhythmically.

At Ida's appearance, the band of two halted suddenly, but the little dancer continued.

"Busi, why do you stop?" came muffled from beneath the lampshade. No reply. The lampshade slowly settled and two brown eyes peered from beneath the shade. *"Eeish!"*

"Sanibonani, little makers of music." Ida stepped into the room and plopped onto the edge of the bed. "Did you sleep well?"

For a moment Moses' eyes crinkled and light flickered behind the smile but faded again into emptiness. Ida studied the child. Why hadn't she seen it before? It was sadness that followed this child like a hungry dog, not shyness. Ida felt the rough hands of pity twist her insides.

13

"Surprise kick me off the bed." Bandile brought Ida back to the present as he tumbled off the bed to demonstrate. Still hugging the lampshade, Surprise hooted with pleasure and collapsed sideways, stamping his feet.

Bandile righted himself, grinning.

Ida smiled, then said, "Bandile, where do you live?"

"Up there," his hand flapped in the direction of up-river.

That was helpful. She tried again. "How did you get here?"

"We run after Busi." His chin jutted in Moses' direction. Ida took in the name.

"She was in the blue box?"

He nodded. "She was hide in the box and the heavy water come quickly, and *whsssh*." His hand shot out to show the sudden departure of the box. "She is gone."

"Were you playing a game?"

He shook his head slowly. "Ah, no." His smile disappeared. He shuffled closer to Moses who watched him pick at his toenails. Surprise was now holding the burglar bars at the window and gazing outside, his feet thudding against the wall, humming softly to himself.

"Why…?" She never finished. The buzzer sounded at the gate. Her watch said 8:00 a.m.

"That'll be Simeon." She dashed to the kitchen, checked the gate then pressed the buzzer to let him in. She unlocked the kitchen door and watched as he bounded through the gate. Recently, each Saturday he'd come, he seemed to have grown. "You know what, Simeon? I think you'll be six feet before your next birthday." Ida stared up at him.

The teenager stretched himself to his full height and his guileless black face beamed. "Good morning, Mrs. Morgan."

"Morning, Simeon. How did your Math test go this week?"

"It's okay," he smiled. "It's easy when you explain to me how to do it."

"I'm glad. Before you start work in the garden today, I want you to meet someone." Simeon wiped his feet on the mat and followed her into the spare room. He swung round to Ida, his eyebrows reaching new heights when he saw the children.

"*Hawu?*" he said inspecting them in turn.

14

Ida faced Simeon. "I need you to help me find out where these children live." Simeon listened as she filled him in on what had happened.

"I'll make breakfast then I'm off to the shops to buy some things for the children. Please stay with them until I get back."

He nodded and slid down next to Moses and stuck out his hand. "*Sawubona*, I am Simeon." Moses, still hugging her knees gave him the tips of her fingers but wouldn't look at him.

"Busi doesn't speak," Ida said. "I call her Moses." She placed a hand on each of the boys. "This is Bandile and Surprise." She moved off to get her handbag.

Ida returned an hour later, hauling a collection of plastic bags, weighed down and threatening to burst at the seams. She heaved them onto the kitchen table, then reaching over the faux granite countertop she switched on the kettle. Tea made the world go round and when it didn't, it made you go round, so it didn't matter so much the world had stopped. From the kitchen she heard murmuring in the spare room and wondered if Simeon had been more successful than she had.

After putting on a pot of oatmeal to simmer, she sorted the groceries into two piles. One of the piles she tucked into her cupboards, the rest she repacked into the bags. Then slowing down she peered into the bags she hadn't touched yet.

"Mrs. Morgan?"

Her head snapped up.

"I think I know where the children's house is." Simeon stood in the doorway moving his weight from one leg to the other. "They are on the other side of K4. It is between the new graveyard and the stream. Near the old farm house."

"Will you be able to explain it to the policeman?"

"Why do you want the police?"

"They will take the children home."

Simeon frowned. "But I think you will take them."

Ida stared back. "I can't take them. I don't know where to go. I'll get lost."

"I can show you."

"But it's not safe." She turned away from him and picked up a plate from the drying rack and slammed it on top of the stacked dinner plates in the cupboard.

Simeon backed away.

"I shouldn't have done that. I'm so sorry." She extended her hand to him. "It's not your fault."

"Mrs. Morgan, it is the day. I will go with you."

"You don't understand. I can't take them."

"It is not too far."

"Simeon, I heard two of the men who killed my husband live in Masoyi. They were never caught." Her shoulders sagged. When would she get rid of this porcupine of fear that dogged her day and night? How could she stop embracing its quills and be free?

"Ah. Sorry. Sorry." Simeon shook his head.

"Please, Mama." Bandile's serious face appeared suddenly from behind Simeon and scooted in front of him. Moses and Surprise followed, squeezing in on either side of Simeon in the doorway.

Moses extended her arm and shook Bandile's shoulder, pointing to Ida. Bandile looked up at his sister. She nodded. He fixed his gaze on Ida. "No policeman," he said. Without taking his eyes off hers he sidled up to her and slipped his hand into hers. "Please, Mama."

"Did you do something wrong?" Ida said softly.

"Ah, no."

She tightened her grasp on the little hand and felt the familiar buzzing in her head. The tug between fear and responsibility and as usual fear had the stronger grip. She was damned if she did and damned if she didn't.

"I'll think about it." She turned to the bags on the counter afraid the children could read her face. "Come and eat; then I'll show you what I have here."

After breakfast the children stared blankly at the clothes on the counter. "They're for you." Ida said. She picked up a simple cotton dress and pressed it up against Moses. "See," she said, picking out the clusters of roses like tiny bouquets printed on it, "Flowers for a special little rose."

Moses' eyes filled with tears. She picked up the dress and pressed it against her. Then, reaching up, she looped her arms around Ida's neck and squeezed. Ida's arms slowly circled the child and squeezed back. Her eyes closed–her first hug in nearly two years. For several seconds they stood there and Ida wondered when last this child had

16

been cuddled. She smiled down at her and stroked the smooth young cheek. "Let's see how the boys are doing."

Bandile stood in the centre of the kitchen wearing his new T-shirt and shorts. Ida watched him raise the picture on the shirt. He stretched it away from his eyes, squinting. He twisted it this way and that, frowning, then pulled the shirt over his head. At arms length and still with narrowed eyes he stared at the figure on the shirt. Still he couldn't see. He placed the shirt carefully on the back of the kitchen chair and moved back a few paces. The frown disappeared as he studied the picture. "What is this?" he said.

"It's Spiderman."

"I do not like spiders."

Ida moved closer to him. How could she explain? "He is a good man who helps people. He's not..." Too complicated. Maybe another time. She disappeared into the bedroom and returned with a pair of her generic reading glasses. She eased them onto his face and pushed him closer to the shirt.

"Is that better?"

The smile said it all.

"You may keep them. They will help you read or see something close up."

"I can see." He snatched up Moses' hand. "Look, I can see." Dragging her round the room he stared into the mirror, touched the wall hanging, traced the pattern in the curtain, fingered the lace cloth under the table lamp.

What profound consequences for such a small act. Ida reveled in the pleasure of it.

When Bandile reached Simeon he stopped. "Now I am a man." He flexed his muscles.

Simeon bent forward and, with his thumb and forefinger, pressed the boy's arm. "Yes," he said without smiling. "There are big muscles hiding in there. Feed them and give them some hard work and they will come out big and strong."

A commotion behind her brought Ida's attention to Surprise. He was David in Goliath's clothes. The T-shirt fit but no sooner would he grab one side of the red shorts to hold them up then the other side would droop to his ankles. Where was that sewing kit? This was something a large safety pin could sort out–for now anyway. It wouldn't be noticeable if she pulled them in at the back. One good thing though was that he could grow into those shorts–if they didn't wear out before then.

"One more packet." Ida reached into the last bag feeling like Father Christmas and pulled out three pairs of flip-flops. Guessing shoe sizes had been too risky, plus her budget didn't stretch that far– so these simple sandals were a good compromise.

As she inspected the children who stood in a row before her she knew she had to take them home. How quickly the heart expanded when a child charmed his way into it. Perhaps that's what people meant when they talked about what it was like having a child.

It was noon and time to go. Herding them and Simeon into the car with two bags of groceries, Ida reversed her 'Old Lady,' a 1992 Mazda 323 out the gate and pressed the small black-and-grey remote in her hand. She waited while the heavy wrought-iron gate rattled closed behind her. Sure that no one was hanging around outside the fence, she flicked the gear stick into first.

She turned into Jacaranda Drive. The tires crunched and spat loose gravel on the unpaved road. The houses stood on one acre plots of land giving Ida a glimpse of the stream that ran parallel to the street on the northern side. She was about to drive past the Van Reenens next door when she made the car squeal to a stop.

"I'm just going to see if the neighbors have seen my cat. Won't be long." She jumped out the car and rang the bell at the filigreed iron gate. The voice of Gladys, the maid, answered. She waited a minute while Gladys went to find out if anyone had seen the cat. They hadn't. Ida thanked her and jumped back into car.

"Simeon, you'll need to guide me once we're on the Numbi Gate road." She eased the car back onto Jacaranda Drive, then hung a right into Springbok Road. In the rearview mirror she could see the children. Moses sat on the driver's side with her arm resting on Surprise's shoulders—her face expressionless but her eyes working overtime. Bandile sat forward, holding the door pull with one hand, his right hand gripped the headrest in front of him. He stared at the world whizzing by.

Onto the main road toward Numbi Gate. The first ten kilometers of well-maintained road was mostly forestry and farm land sprinkled with a few houses. As they approached the outer area of Masoyi, Ida slowed down. How often had she driven past Masoyi to get to the Kruger Game Park and never taken any notice of the enormous community that lived there?

She looked with new eyes. Wave upon wave of two or three-roomed homes, made of large grey concrete bricks, dotted the rolling hills of the countryside. A small patch of compacted earth surrounded each house, swept clean and neat with the occasional tiny garden or a banana tree growing in the yard or some *mama* hanging her washing on a fence that was strong enough to hold it. She snuck a glance at Simeon. This was his world.

He leaned forward in his seat and pointed to a large unused quarry just off the road on the right.

"I play there when I am small."

"You live near here?" Ida asked.

"Yes, on the other side of the hill." He thought for a moment then said, "When I am maybe five years, my friend Sipho and me play in the hole where the men take sand for building houses. One day we find a big tin bath. We take it to the top of the hole and we get in the bath. Me first, then Sipho. Then we ride down to the bottom of the hill."

"Sounds like fun."

"Yes, but one day a big *mama* see us." His young voice cracked as it ascended to womanly heights. "'*Eeish,*' she say, 'What you bad boys doing with my bath? I have look everywhere for it.'

"We look at her. We look at the bath and we know there is trouble. We say, 'Sorry. Sorry. Here is your bath.' She pick up the bath and hold it in the air. 'Why I can see the sky through the bottom of my bath?' She throw down the bath and chase us. She shout, 'Bad boys. Bad boys.'"

"Did she catch you?" Ida asked.

"No. She make so much noise a dog bark at her. She doesn't stop. The dog doesn't stop. She turn right around and run the other way. 'Bad dog. Bad dog,' she shout. The dog, he chase her all the way home."

Ida laughed. For a moment it reminded her of childhood home in KwaZulu-Natal. Happy times of discovery and learning about anything that grew or moved or changed. "When I was a little girl," she said, "my Uncle Ken showed me a grasshopper that had ears in its knees." she said.

The children looked sideways at her and said, "*Hawu?*"

"You don't believe me? It's true. Uncle Ken knew every jumper, creeper, crawler, stalker, hopper, stomper, and snorter in the bush." The children listened. "He showed me so many wonderful things. I made a scrapbook and wrote inside it all the things I learned."

She still had her *Oddities and Weirdities* book. It was what brought her and Tony together when they met in the Zoology department on the first day of her first semester at UCT in Cape Town. "Both our dreams eventually came true. He became a teacher. I became his wife." She suddenly realized she'd spoken aloud and felt a warming in her cheeks. She was spared more embarrassment when Simeon said, "After the chicken man, you turn there." He directed her left with a flick of his hand.

The chicken man stood next to a makeshift shelter of gum poles and tattered plastic sheets half covering the roof. Under it leaned a wire-mesh cage holding an assortment of hens. The man drank from an old tin cup, apparently unconcerned by the discomfort of so many birds crammed together so feathers and tails protruded through the wire netting.

Ida slowed to a crawl and eased the car over the four-inch drop off at the edge of tarred road and swung onto a rough dirt track sandwiched between two rows of houses. She surveyed the road she was supposed to go on. How was she supposed to take the Old Lady over that obstacle course of dongas and mounds? If she didn't get a puncture, she'd get stuck in the mud that hadn't quite dried since the storm and lay in wait to snag unsuspecting vehicles.

Did people actually drive along here? She dropped her head on the steering wheel. "I can't do this," she whispered. The chatting in the car stopped. Silence. She raised her head and looked around her. To her right, two men sat in the shade of a stunted acacia tree watching her. On the other side of the road a large woman carrying a bucket on her head glanced their way as she walked past. Even a stray dog, dragging his body of bones around with him, ceased his endless sniffing for food to stare at her.

In the mirror she took in the wide eyes of the children and she knew she had to go on. "You sure it's not far from here?"

"It will not take long now." Simeon said. "When we pass those houses at the top of the hill, we will be nearly there."

Ida set off again, keeping abreast of a young boy navigating his home-made wire car before him, head up and weaving his body in time with the music in his mind. A yelp from the back seat brought her attention to the children being thrown from side to side by violent twists and turns as she negotiated the impossible track. "Hang on, everyone," she spun the wheel sharply to the left to avoid the undercarriage of the car being impaled on a jagged rock protruding from the ground.

"Some other roads are not as bad as this," Simeon said, his knuckles white on the dashboard.

"Lucky me."

The track became steeper but as it neared the brow of the hill, the frequency of houses and people thinned out.

"The graveyard is on the other side of the hill," Simeon said, leaning forward to keep his watch for potholes.

"Then how far is it?"

"I think it is after the old farm house near the bottom of the hill."

Cresting the hill, Ida saw the cemetery. The hill flattened out into a plateau the size of a rugby field. She felt some of the tension leave her when she realized there were no visitors to the gravesites. She slid the gears into neutral and pulled the emergency brake. As she rolled down the window to get a better look, a blast of blistering heat rushed in. At the same time a wave of sadness hit her as she scanned the cemetery. Most of the graves were as fresh as her own grief. The mounds of earth had not yet sunk level with the ground.

Some sites were marked with a neat pile of stones, others by two short wooden planks sunk into the ground and a piece of board hammered to them with the name and date of the deceased written on it. Some were marked with a rough rectangle of bricks. Others had a rough wooden cross driven into the earth. Each concealed a story and none had a happy ending.

Enough of that. Ida thrust Old Lady back into gear and eased forward. The track bypassed the cemetery as she drove to the end of the plateau and began the downward journey. Halfway down the hill to the right, she could see the broken shell of the old farm house. The remains of jagged walls, blackened from fire, protruded through overgrown weeds and rubble.

Beyond that, there were no more buildings until the bottom of the hill. There, a cluster of umbrella thorn trees circled three of the same small grey houses she'd passed along the road. Shade from the trees spread a large canopy of shadows under the glare of the burning sun.

The track they were on petered out a short distance beyond where they were parked and became a path meandering through the tall elephant grass. She became aware the children had stopped talking. "Is one of those houses yours?" she asked.

All three children sat upright, craning their necks to see the small group of houses. When no one answered, Ida turned around briefly to face them. Moses pointed to the one on the far right.

"Then you are home." Ida laughed. There was no response. Strange. Her rear view mirror showed all three children slumped back against the car seat, their faces expressionless.

Right now she needed to back off the sloping mound of rock she had driven the front tires onto. She thrust the lever into reverse. Then, without warning, she felt the left front tire slip on a patch of sand and slide sideways off the slope landing with a bouncing thud into a hole. The car stalled. Ida turned the key and pressed the accelerator. The wheels whined and spun, churning out clouds of dust. Please. Not here.

She jumped out the car. "Help me push the car out," she said to Simeon. The two of them began to push from the front when the passenger side door opened and Moses, followed by the two boys, scrambled out and lent their weight. The wheel bumped repeatedly against the ledge of rock at both ends of the hole and stayed put.

Bending down, Ida could see the problem. The car had fallen into a deep depression in the surface of the rock. It was circular, like the top edge of a large bucket and deep enough to hem the tire in on all sides. Maybe if they filled the small space behind the wheel with bits of grass and twigs it would provide enough traction to move it out when she accelerated.

The children and Simeon went running off to find what they could. Then, together, they heaved against the front of the car while she sat behind the wheel and flattened the accelerator. But the tire just spewed out the grass and twigs and thumped against the face of the hole.

Ida switched off and climbed out. She leaned against the car shading her eyes against the glare of the sun and wiped the back of her hand across her forehead. It would take more than five lightweights to move the car.

Then her eyes brightened as she had a thought. Of course. The jack. "We're okay," she said and opened the boot. "We'll hoist the car up and..." She scratched around. Where was it? It had to be there. She let the lid slam shut. It came rushing back to her. Cindy from next door had borrowed it and hadn't returned it.

Simeon stepped over to her. "Mrs. Morgan, I will go and find someone to help us."

She glanced at her watch. The thudding of her heart eased a little when she saw that it was still only one thirty. She nodded. "I'll walk the kids home then meet you back here." Once more she opened the boot of the car and pulled out the grocery bags. From the top of a pile of old newspapers she pulled a newspaper plus a two-liter bottle of water which she handed to Moses to carry and then locked the car behind her. "Let's go kids."

From this height she could see where the narrow trail led but once they'd left the track and were on the path, their vision was obscured by grass on either side, six feet high. It became a maze, taking away the security of seeing where they were going. Without a doubt she wouldn't be doing this if she hadn't seen where the path led from up there.

She fell into the rhythm of walking, the bags bumping the sides of her legs. In the stillness, she could hear the swish of the children walking behind her. First Surprise, then Bandile, with Moses bringing up the rear. She was grateful they were descending the hill rather than climbing it on such a hot day. Her mind wandered to the children. Why no enthusiasm for being home? Perhaps the parents worked and wouldn't be home to greet them.

Her thoughts were interrupted by an overpowering stench. After moving around a kink in the path they came upon a dog lying across it a short distance in front of them. Flies in their hundreds settled around the exposed areas of the lifeless body while a myriad of ants moved in and out of decaying openings. Ida slapped her hand to her nose in an attempt to reduce the nauseating smell that made her eyes smart.

"Let's get out of here." She lowered the bags, rubbed her red flattened fingers and stood aside to let the children pass. Bandile put his glasses on and bent over the carcass. "Ahh!" He jerked his head back, pinched his nose and hurried on. Moses turned her head away and walked quickly past. There was no further comment. Ida guessed this was probably not new to them.

She grabbed the groceries, beginning to wish she'd left them in the car and picked up the pace. It was a few minutes before they moved out of range of the smell. The encounter with the dog brought back the realization that she needed to watch more carefully where she was going. Along almost the entire stretch of the path, discarded papers and bags of all kinds littered the path. Shredded plastic caught in the grass and flapped in the breeze. They needed to step around shriveled orange and banana peels that spilled out of ripped black bags and mingled with rusty cans.

They passed the farmhouse on the right as they followed the path on its meandering way downwards. Quite suddenly the path forked ahead of them. Moses hurried past her brothers to Ida and tapped her on the shoulder. Moses dipped her head, indicating they should take the path that turned right. Ida realized with shock she hadn't seen the fork from the car. What else had she missed from up there?

The difference between this path and the one they'd just been on was marked. She observed very little litter and noticed the path floor had not been trampled down to sand. These three families did not have many visitors.

As the soil was becoming shallower and stonier, the grass grew shorter, making it easier to see where they were going. Ida stopped and lowered the bags once more. She rummaged in the pocket of her skirt for a tissue to wipe her face. She would sometimes joke she should never have been born in Africa. She hated being in the fierce sun. This feeling of stickiness and the fine grey dust that produced rashes on her fair skin were too irritating to ignore. Give her winter anytime.

As they neared the group of houses at the bottom of the hill, the path all but disappeared and the party picked its way through scrubby thorn trees and straggly bushes. Ida stepped aside. "Moses, you lead the way." Moses drew abreast of Ida and stopped, lowering the bottle of water. She stretched upward, peering through foliage and listened. The boys stood silently behind her. No welcome home.

"So where is everyone?"

Then Moses was running into the clearing. To the first house she charged, banging on the door with a grubby hole where the door handle was meant to be. No answer. She ran across the dirt courtyard, past the open fire pit to the next house identical to the first. Again she hammered on the door, and pulled the handle down but it didn't budge. Lastly, she ran to the house she had pointed out as being theirs. The door was ajar. She stopped to listen. Slowly she approached and disappeared inside. When she didn't reappear immediately, Ida turned to Bandile.

"What's going on? Where are your parents?"

He shrugged his shoulder. "They are dead." He took Surprise's hand and together they walked after Moses.

CHAPTER 3

Japie van Reenen pulled away from the window. That woman! He patted his pockets for his cigarettes then picked up a silver lighter from the small mahogany table next to him. His eyes narrowed as the smoke curled into his face. He turned back to watch. What was she doing? For two years now she looked as though she'd sold her smile for a lemon. What a grump.

He craned his neck to see past his kidney-shaped swimming pool to his neighbor's back door through a gap in the hibiscus hedge. No! Were those black kids? He'd have to talk to her about keeping the servant's kids on the property. You never knew what they'd get up to while you were out.

He counted three of them and a bigger boy who looked like he could be her gardener. The children and Lemon moved out of eyesight, and Japie heard a car starting up. Just his luck to be living next to some goodie-goodie. The car moved into the street and the engine died but Japie already had his eyes on something else.

His focus moved from the garden next door to the window itself. Bending forward, he inspected a faint smudge at eye level. "Gladys. Come here." Within seconds he heard footsteps scurrying behind him. "Look at this." He turned to face a woman wearing a pink uniform with ethnic patterned sleeves and hems. "Look at me." The woman raised her head, fingering the dusting cloth in her hands.

"When are you going to learn to clean properly? I don't pay you to sit on your rear-end all day." He jabbed at the smudge on the window.

"Sorry, Master."

Gladys scurried out and came back with a damp cloth. She waited for him to move aside.

Just then, Japie heard the back door open and his face softened. "*Wie is dit*? Is it my little angel?" A toddler came charging in, her light brown curls wet and bouncing as her chubby legs propelled her straight into Japie's open arms.

"Papa, Papa. *Ek kan nou swem*, I can swim now."

Japie picked up the child who all but disappeared beneath his bulky arms. He pressed her to him, smelling the chlorine in her hair. "So you are no longer my little angel; you're my little fish? You've been learning lots of things in your swimming lessons?" The child pushed against his chest to be let down.

"Come and watch me." She grabbed his hand and tried to pull him toward the front door.

"Later, *my skat*. The big storm we had the other night blew lots of leaves and rubbish into the pool. When Edward has cleaned it, I'll take you for swim." He looked to the front door. "Where's your mom?"

Just then, Rene van Reenen entered through the front door, closing the carved rosewood door behind her. She dropped her leather bag and car keys onto the ornate telephone table in the entrance way. "You'll scratch the table if you throw the keys down like that." Japie could not keep the irritation out of his voice.

Rene flicked aside a tendril of light brown hair from her eyes with slim, well-manicured fingers, drew a deep breath and spoke to the child. "Estelle, did you tell your dad it won't be long before you can swim without armbands?"

The child nodded.

Japie watched them go—the two bright lights in his life. He knew he could be hard on them but you did what was right for the family. They didn't have to like it.

The gate buzzer sounded. "Gladys, see who that is." Gladys appeared a few minutes later. "The madam from next door says have you seen her ginger cat? She has not seen it after the bad storm."

"Which madam?"

"Mrs. Morgan."

"No, I haven't."

Gladys had started back to Mrs. Morgan when Rene emerged from the bathroom, holding a large white towel. "I heard a cat crying in a tree near the stream earlier this morning."

"Was it her cat?" Japie asked, his voice sharp. Rene stared at him. "I don't know. I was a bit late getting Estelle to swimming lessons so I had to go."

"Then tell the madam we don't know where her cat is."

"Yes, *Baas*." Gladys hesitated, then left, and Rene took a long look at Japie and returned to Estelle in the bathroom.

Japie lowered his tanned body onto a beige leather couch, adjusting the rust and red cushion. Then, he picked up the *Saturday Star* from the well-polished coffee table. He hooked a small red ottoman with his shoe and heaved it in front of him and raised his feet onto it. He tried to lean back. These ridiculous modern things. The lounge suite was going back on Monday. You couldn't rest your head on the back of it. Why had he allowed Rene to buy it?

"Gladys. Bring me some tea."

He looked up as Gladys came in a short while later. She carried a tray with cup and saucer, milk jug and a teapot being kept warm by a plump brocade and lace tea cozy. She placed it on the side table next to him.

"My wife said she saw police at Mrs. Morgan's house yesterday. Do you know why?" he asked.

She shrugged her shoulders. "I don't know, *Baas.*"

Japie's gaze moved over to the pool. He studied Edward's efforts to clean the pool. Man, was he slow. Japie snapped out of the chair and marched over to the window. "Edward!"

The man looked up.

"Don't forget to lock the pool gate when you're finished."

The man nodded and mumbled something Japie could not hear.

Japie went back to his paper. On the front page, he saw the picture of a man bloodied and beaten after he'd violently ripped a woman's cell phone away from her. Bystanders had jumped in and were providing roadside justice when the police arrived just in time to save the man's life.

"About time someone did something about all the crime."

Japie was halfway through the business section when Rene called from the bathroom. "Japie, please watch Estelle for me. I just want to wash my own hair quickly. I won't be long."

"*Ja*, okay." Japie picked up the paper once more. He felt little fingers pat his arm.

"Papa. Come play with me."

"In a minute, *my skattie*. Just let Daddy finish reading the paper, then I'll come and play with you." The little hands lifted, and somewhere in his consciousness he heard the gentle slap of bare feet receding from the room. He was soon lost in the world of the Stock Exchange.

"Estelle?" Rene's voice broke through his thoughts. "*Waar is jy?* Where are you?"

"For goodness sake, Rene. Do you have to shout?"

"Where is Estelle?"

"She was here a minute ago."

He felt Rene's long nails dig into his arm. "Japie, I can't find Estelle."

"She's got to be here somewhere. She can't just disappear." He went back to his newspaper. Edward was at the pool if she'd gone there.

The pool gate. He'd heard it squeak!

Suddenly Japie threw down his paper, leapt out his chair and dashed over to the window. "Edward! Edward!"

No answer.

The pool gate was ajar.

No Edward.

He flung open the front door and tore outside.

CHAPTER 4

Ida watched the boys disappear inside their home and wished lightning would strike her dead. She hadn't asked them anything about themselves. Just presumed. There were indicators but she'd missed them–all. How could she be so insensitive? This was way beyond her.

She stood in the courtyard looking around, but seeing nothing. What was she supposed to do now? She came to with a start when Moses brushed past her and ran to what Ida supposed was the communal longdrop. The unvarnished wooden door, without handle or lock, resisted Moses' pushing and screeched as it grated against the concrete floor. Moses heaved it far enough to look inside.

Ida slapped her fingers against her nostrils and turned her face away. Then, when Moses left without finding what she wanted, Ida took a deep breath, reached in, grabbed the door and tugged it shut.

"What are you looking for, Moses?"

Moses turned her hand upside down, palm up, and brought it level with her thigh. Ida gasped. She knew the sign. There was another child.

"I'll come with you." Ida started off but Moses grabbed her by her skirt. She held up her hands and shook her head.

"But I can help you."

Again the child shook her head.

Okay. Maybe if there was another child he wouldn't come to a stranger. She hurried over to find the boys.

From the doorway of their home she could make out the shape of the two boys sitting banana-backed and heads down at the end of a bare mattress lying against the wall. The small covered window above the bed let in enough light for her to see Surprise pick at the frayed corner of the mattress, pulling out a thin stream of stuffing. He stopped to cough. Next to him Bandile, bent over between his knees, tapped the floor with the back of his knuckles.

Ida stepped across the dusty cement floor and leaned over the boys to pull the curtain aside. She stopped. The curtain was nothing more than a towel hooked up by two bent nails to cover the window. Through the worn areas crept patches of weak light. There was no way she could move it without it falling apart in her hands. She left it alone.

Straightening, she glanced down as a slight movement at her feet caught her eye. A large rain spider scuttled past her and disappeared under the only other piece of furniture in the room, an embattled three-drawer dresser. She jumped back, her heart pounding. Spiders should swap places with the dodo.

With her eyes on the bottom of the dresser, she spoke to Bandile. "Moses says there's another child. Is that right?"

Bandile's head twisted round to look at her. "*Yebo*. There is more."

"Would you help Moses find him?" He got up slowly and walked out. With one last glare at the dresser, Ida took Surprise's hand and followed Bandile into the sunshine. She searched for the deepest part of the umbrella thorn's shade and sat down cross-legged on the stony soil. Hefting Surprise onto her lap, she waited. The child leaned against her and started humming.

"You love to sing don't you, Surprise?" He swung his head around to look up at her and slid his arms around her neck. His body tensed and he bowed over, his small body shuddering with fierce coughing. She rubbed his back. She had to find a way to get him some medication.

Into her line of vision came Bandile. Drawing level with the fire-pit, he cupped his hand around his mouth. "Promise. Zinhle. Phineas. Samson. Agnus. *Kulungile*. Come here."

There was more than one?

Moses came running up and stood beside him.

He spoke into the bushes again. "*Mama* Morgan is here. She will not hurt you." They stopped to listen. In the silence, disturbed only by the occasional ruffling of leaves through the thorn trees, Ida became aware of her own breathing. Even that sounded loud.

She snatched a look up the hill. Still no sign of Simeon.

The moment, broken by her movement, sent Bandile off again, shouting as he ran and followed by Moses. As they reached the second house, they split up and sprinted around it, reappearing near a thicket of bushes that grew between the last two houses. Behind the bushes stood a mound of earth like a giant anthill. Here they halted and peered into the dense brush.

They glanced at each other and Moses nodded.

"It is safe," Bandile said, his voice gentle. "You can come." After

31

several seconds, the bushes began to stir with a crackle and a swish of twigs. The foliage closest to the children parted and a young face appeared–eyes huge and searching. Slowly the rest of him followed. He was about eleven. He crept out onto the sand, followed by a small boy clutching the back of his shirt and treading on his heels.

"Come," he said to the younger child, twisting around to haul the quivering child next to him. The child held on tight, his face hidden.

She was so engrossed in watching this little episode that Ida hadn't noticed three more children—each younger than the first— sneak out of the bushes until she heard a squeal. All the children threw themselves upon each other in a tangled ball of legs and arms. Her brief moment of concern turned to relief when she identified laughter amongst the tears.

Then, as if on cue, the mass of little bodies fell apart and the group began a rowdy verbal exchange, but Ida found it difficult to follow when they all yelled their news at the same time and no one listened. For a few minutes she studied this group of little people who could laugh together when they should cry. A strange warmth filled her from her feet up.

The celebration continued but suddenly she felt the odd man out, like a postman interrupting a close family gathering. She was an interloper here. She felt the porcupine backing into her. Where was Simeon? He should have been back ages ago.

Finally the noise of the children diminished. One by one they turned to face her.

"*Sanibonani,*" she said.

"*Yebo, Sawubona.*" The older boy answered the greeting almost inaudibly.

"My name is Mrs. Morgan. I have brought your friends home." The children stared back. Whenever she caught a child's eye, they looked elsewhere.

"What are your names?" When no one responded, Bandile positioned them in a line. Starting with the oldest boy he said, "This is Samson. He catch a rat this big." He stretched his arms wide.

"Hmm. The size of a warthog?" Ida said.

"Ah, no." He grinned and reduced the size of the rat. He continued, "His brother, he is Phineas. They live there." He indicated the first house. He moved over to the girls. "This is Promise and she's sisters, Zinhle and Agnus. This is they house."

"Where are your parents?" she said, but she already knew the answer.

The oldest boy dragged his toe through the sand, making a circle in front of him. He said, "Our parents they are dead." He nodded in Moses' direction. "Busi, she is *Mama* for us."

"*Ncesi*. Excuse me. I need to think for a minute." Ida hoisted Surprise off her lap and scrambled to her feet. She disappeared around the umbrella thorn. Clutching her mouth, she bent over, desperate to keep from howling. She stopped and scowled into the sky.

"What did they do to deserve all this?" she flung her arm in the children's direction. "How could you do this to them?" She was on a roll. God was never around when you needed him. "Look up there." Stabbing a finger toward her vehicle she continued. "My car's trapped in a hole. Simeon has disappeared. There's a bunch of kids living here without anyone caring for them. What am I supposed to do? Are you even listening to me?" She became aware that her voice had risen, and peeped around the tree. Eight pairs of eyes stared at her. She swung back and pressed against the trunk until she felt the rough shavings of bark gnaw at her back.

She closed her eyes. Breathe in and out. Slower. In and out. As her tension began to dissipate, her eyes strayed up the hill. She straightened. She hadn't noticed that woman walking down the path toward her, carrying a bulging, blue-and-red nylon bag.

The woman drew near the fork in the path. She caught sight of Ida and paused. "*Sawubona, Mama.* Is that your car up there?" she called.

Ida nodded. "*Sawubona. Yebo.* It's stuck on the rock."

"You must be careful. Some people near the road are very angry."

Her pulse began to throb. "What happened?"

"The bus drivers they have been on strike for three weeks. The people are angry because they cannot get to work. No work. No money." She lowered her burden onto the path in front of her. "Just now a man try to stop a bus but it hit him. Now some young men they are throwing stones at the cars. They are bad boys. They make lots of trouble in Masoyi."

"*Ngiyabonga.* I thank you for letting me know. *Humba kahle.* Go well."

The woman smiled, "*Sala kahle*." She picked up her bag and was about to continue down the path when Ida had a thought.

"*Mama*, did you pass a young man wearing a red shirt and yellow cap on your way here?"

"I have not seen him." The woman moved on.

Four o'clock and Simeon still hadn't arrived. Ida scratched around in her bag for her cell phone. She knew two things. She wasn't staying here tonight and she wasn't leaving the kids on their own. Sally down the road from her house had a VW Beetle, but that would be way too small for all of them. Don had a Mazda bakkie but he was in Mozambique for the week. Of course, Japie van Reenen from next door had a van but she'd rather be bitten by a *boomslang* than ask him.

She continued down the list of people she knew but there was no one else who could help her. What about a taxi? She added up the cost of eight children and an adult. As it was, she didn't know how she was going to pay the R500 for car repairs and Dr. Oosthuizen's bill for her last visit. Plus the likelihood of getting them all into one taxi van was close to nil.

The more she thought about it, the more Japie van Reenen looked like the best option. Maybe his bite was worse than his poison. She dialed his number.

"Hello, Mr. van Reenen. It's Ida Morgan from next door."

"Hello? Hello?"

"Mr. van Reenen, It's…"

"Hello?"

The line went dead. Ida stared down at the battery icon on her phone. No bars. Why hadn't she recharged her battery last night when she'd thought of it? Something struck her. If anyone came for them, they would have to get by the angry mob over the hill. That risk wasn't worth taking.

Ida returned to the children. Moses crouched in front of the fire pit, blowing into the beginnings of an insubstantial fire sandwiched between two bricks. Balanced on the bricks sat an aluminum pot. "What are you making?" Ida, realizing how hungry she was, peered into the pot. It held a small amount of water. She plopped down onto the sand next to Samson.

"She is cooking water." Samson sat on a green plastic chair, holding the front page of the newspaper, some of which Moses had used to start the fire. He did not look up. Mouth moving, a frown on his face, she could hear him sound out words under his breath.

"What is she going to cook?"

Samson continued reading.

"Samson?"

Samson glanced over at the listless children sprawled on the ground on the far side of the fire, neither chatting nor moving. He lowered his voice, "When there is no food she cook the water. The small children think there is food coming so they wait. When they sleep we take them to bed."

Could things get any worse? Ida scrambled up and ran to the plastic bags under the tree. "I brought you some food," she said, scratching around in a bag.

Every child sat up. Alert. She hauled out a five kilogram bag of maize meal and a can of tomatoes with onions, and placed them next to the fire. "Moses, is there another pot to heat the tomatoes? Oh, and Promise, we need a spoon for stirring the pap."

Samson carefully placed the newspaper cutting on the chair before streaking off and calling the other children to help him find more sticks for the fire. Promise disappeared to find a spoon. She reappeared a minute later, carrying a large wooden one.

Ida looked around her. "We need more water. Where is the tap, Moses?"

"We get water from the river and sometimes from the rain." Promise spoke up for the first time. Ida rushed over to the water bottle to see how much water was left after the children had all helped themselves to it. Only a few mouths' full. "Do you have any water anywhere?"

"I have water." Promise ran off into her house and reappeared with a plastic container with about two liters of water in it. "I get it when it rain."

Ida opened the lid and peered in. It looked a little brown but didn't smell bad. If they boiled it for a while it should kill off any *goggas* that might be lurking in it. Moses found a small enamel pot whose sides were still encrusted with the leftovers of the last meal. She picked out the larger pieces of dehydrated food and then threw sand

35

into the pot. Wetting the sand with a little water she scoured the pot clean. A swizzle of water and the pot was rinsed and ready to use.

Bandile returned with an armful of twigs and dry grass, scraps of paper, cow dung and buck droppings. He danced into the courtyard, his shuffling feet rising and falling in time to a spontaneous song. "Today we will eat till our stomachs are full."

Behind him, the other children followed, their hands full of kindling. Taking up the refrain, they thumped their feet in the sand and moved in a line as one.

One at a time they dropped the firewood in front of the fire then continued to dance around the fire pit their voices raised, their bodies twisting and winding to the rhythm of their clapping.

When the food was cooked, Moses and Ida served the pap and tomato relish into a motley collection of plates and bowls that Promise had arranged on the plastic chair and on the log next to it. As each plate filled with food it was snatched away by hungry hands, until one plate remained for Ida.

The wooden spoon she tried to eat with proved too cumbersome. Throwing it down she attacked the food in the same way she saw the children do, molding small amounts of the stiff maize meal porridge in her fingers and dipping it into the relish.

When the last of the pap was eaten off the sides of the pot and each plate licked clean enough for the next meal, the younger children ran off to play—except for Phineas. The boy returned to the pots and plates, searching for one last morsel to eat. One by one, he ran his hand over each plate. He peered into the pot, feeling for lumps that may have been missed. When he uncovered no hidden treasure, he too ran off.

Ida stroked the little head that rested in her lap. Within seconds she felt Surprise's body go limp in sleep.

By five-thirty Ida knew Simeon wasn't coming back. She was going to have to stay here overnight. Images of *panga*-wielding men creeping through the darkness and bursting upon her and the children flashed though her mind, sucking out the innards of reality and leaving her powerless to think clearly. She was desperate. She knew only too well how these thoughts could derail her emotions. She tried to reign in her galloping thoughts. If she lost this battle tonight she'd never win her private war.

In the middle of her confusion she thought of her mother, whose own body had failed her in every way except to keep breathing and whose life was littered with broken dreams. Yet the light in her eyes had been untainted by discouragement or bitterness. "Life is not a battle," she would say. "It's a choice. Make the right choices and the battle becomes a challenge you can overcome."

Even as Ida sat there stroking Surprise's soft curls, she knew the choice she faced was between her wild imagination and truth. Easier said than done, Mom.

It's not a battle, it's a choice. Don't fight it, choose truth. Little by little her emotions calmed like a storm that was spent and her roiling thoughts settled to a manageable level. She knew she still walked a tightrope. If she could just hang onto the choices she made, maybe she'd get out of here in one piece.

Her first test of the evening was finding a light. Sunlight would be gone in an hour. She called to Samson as he ran past.

"Do you have a lamp?"

He spun round. "No. But the moon she is getting big."

It was true. It was almost full moon and it would rise just before the sun set. Together with starlight it would be bright enough to see what they were doing.

Surprise stirred and looked around him. He pulled himself up and eased himself into her lap. Conscious of the warm child lying against her, Ida watched the sun take its final measured path behind the rock koppie on the horizon. It slipped away leaving its imprint of amber and gold, and calling the children to return. They filtered back, finding places round the fire.

Samson threw the remaining kindling onto the flames, sending up showering sparks that flickered and fizzled and then tumbled downward. Tiny pinpricks of light fading into twirling black ash.

At first Ida noticed that the children's conversation was subdued, with frequent glances in her direction, but as the evening wore on their voices grew louder and more animated. A gust of wind whipped through the courtyard, agitating the fire and driving before it a cloud of gritty smoke. The conversation ceased as those children in its path scattered to other smoke-free positions.

The fire finally subsided into patches of smoldering coals. The three youngest children all lay where they were, eyes closed, hands tucked under their heads in the sand.

Ida stood up and groaned. She waited for the blood to move through her cramped legs. She bent down and gently lifted Surprise, taking him over to his house. At the doorway she stood aside to let in the little light there was. Allowing her eyes to get used to the darkness, she searched the room for any four or six-legged nighttime visitors that might be making themselves at home. Satisfied, she laid the child on the bed and covered him with the remains of a threadbare blanket.

As she rejoined the children, Samson was speaking in a low voice to Moses. "We cannot stay here. They will come when the moon…" His head snapped up when he noticed Ida listening in.

"Who will come, Samson?"

He looked over to Moses. She stared into the night. Ida moved over to the two children and dropped onto her haunches. "Tell me who will come?"

Both children looked away.

"We cannot say," Samson said.

"Why not?"

"They say they will kill us if we tell."

CHAPTER 5

The man glanced at his watch; fifteen more minutes before his shift ended. His colleague was deep in conversation with an old lady who had come in with a complaint. No one else waited in line. He picked up a key that was attached to a block of wood by a mangled piece of wire and bearing the word "Men" on it, scooped up his belongings from his locker, and disappeared into the men's room. Three minutes later he emerged, wearing a new set of clothing. He slipped out the back door and sauntered out to his rusty VW.

He needed to check on the little dung beetles before his clients went to visit them at full moon this Friday. Tonight was a good time. He unlocked the car and folded himself inside. From out of his back pocket he pulled the tempting page of adverts from Appliance City, spreading it out on the passenger seat. He devoured the objects of his desire with his eyes. The money he earned from the dung beetles would buy the new flat screen TV on the front page.

On second thoughts, maybe that wasn't such a good idea. His wife would want to know where the money came from.

He sighed and down-scaled his expectations to Plan B. Some new clothes would be good. If he bought them one at a time, she wouldn't notice. In fact, he could tell her he had a raise at work and… his heart began to beat faster. He would give her R20 for Benson's schoolbooks. Then she wouldn't ask where he had got new shoes from.

He switched on the engine, backed out the parking space, and edged toward the line of traffic. A silver Merc 360 came up next and… no, he wasn't letting him in. Too bad. He rolled forward anyway and squeezed between the Merc and the Honda in front. There was no scraping of metal only a long, irate blast on the horn. He watched in his rear view mirror. The Merc had veered to the right to avoid a collision. The driver looked somewhat less than ecstatic. Today was a good day.

The man in the VW snatched a glance at the traffic in front of him. The line of traffic in front of him had moved through the lights. His gaze returned to the mirror. He punched his foot on the brake. The Merc behind him squealed to a stop in a cloud of blue smoke. The VW driver grinned into his rear view mirror. "Having a bad day, sir?" He snapped his hand up to his head in salute and watched for a reaction.

Behind him the Merc driver's arm shot out the window and hammered the air, his face now ruddy and shiny against his white hair. He fumbled to open the door.

Too bad the old man's Merc hadn't rear-ended his car. He could have done with a pay out. He waited for the man in the Merc to step out of the car. Then with a friendly wave, he sped off. In his mirror he saw the white-haired driver shaking a fist at him. He began to whistle. People in new Mercs should be more careful. With wealth comes responsibility. You should know that.

He arrived at the turnoff where the sign said, "Numbi Gate" and waited behind a line of cars turning right. Three cars back sat the silver Merc. Where was the old man going? The gate at Kruger Game Park closed at six so he wouldn't be going there. Plus, this was the long way to Hazyview. It meant one thing. Sorry, old man. If you're looking for a fight you won't be getting it tonight. I have more important business to do. My little dung beetles wait for me.

When he reached the front of the line of cars he found a gap in the traffic and roared down the road, flattening the accelerator. The Merc followed. Interesting. Most people were chicken. They didn't play his little game. They just stamped their expensive shoes and went home. The Merc was gaining on him. Time to hide for a while. He approached the turnoff to Plaston where the side of the road expanded to the left to accommodate slower traffic. Not enough cover. He geared down into third and stormed up the long hill ahead of him.

Approaching the bend at the top of the hill, the man saw two taxi vans parked one behind the other, waiting to offload their passengers.

He geared down and shot around the taxis, skidding to a halt in front of them and scattering the crowd before him. He cut the engine. When the thick cloud of red dust churning around the vehicles settled, and the yells of disenchanted commuters lessened, he started up the engine and inched forward. He waited. The Merc must have passed by now.

Several men came running up to his car and beat on the windows shouting for a ride. Not today. "The buses will be here soon," he yelled, making sure his windows remained closed and the doors locked. He saw they were trying to say something but he feigned ignorance and set off slowly, an eye open for a silver car with a white-haired driver. Five minutes later there it was. Returning. The Merc flew past him so fast he didn't even have time to greet the man.

He leaned back in his seat, flicked on the ancient car radio, and began to sing. His hand thumped the steering wheel in time to the music while his knees bounced in the cramped space beneath it.

His song ended abruptly when, five kilometers before the Numbi Gate turn off, he rounded a bend and confronted a mob of people milling across two lanes of road, shouting and dancing. He hit the brakes. On the shoulder of the road, the burnt out carcass of a Toyota Camry lay on its side, belching clouds of acrid smoke. Fumes from burning tires strewn along the road permeated the air, turning the clear evening air into choking smog. In front, young men prowled like hyenas from one side of the road to the other, gripping large rocks. Waiting to attack… anyone.

So, what had happened today? Bus drivers were on strike but that wasn't enough to cause all this. And he hadn't heard anything at work today. Two young men noticed him and started running toward his car, their arms raised above their heads ready to strike.

He thrust the VW into reverse, swung his body round to look behind him, tires spinning. He heard a mighty thump. His head snapped forward to see what it was. The bottom left hand corner of the windscreen splintered and spread into a spider's web of cracks. A brick-sized rock lurched across the front of the car then slowly tumbled off the side into the road. He felt bile rise into his throat. Another time, another place and that skinny excuse for a man would be joining his ancestors.

He took a second to inspect the windscreen. The splinters had not encroached on his direct line of vision. He floored the pedal. The VW swerved backward in a tight circle in the gravel. He jammed the gear lever into first. Swaying erratically the small car swung onto the road and squealed back the way he had come.

The man slumped in his seat. Watching the scene behind him in the rear view mirror, he saw one of the young men still tearing after his car, yelling and arms flailing.

Too bad. The kids would have to wait. But all the money in the world wasn't worth dying for. Not today anyway. There was still time to get a hold of them before Friday. He slowed down to a crawl and headed home.

41

CHAPTER 6

Simeon waved to Ida then headed back up the way they'd come. Half a minute later, he cleared the brow of the hill and came abreast of the cemetery. Huddled under a tree, deep in conversation, a group of teenage boys caught his attention. This was good. He wouldn't have to go far to get help for the car. He counted five of them. That should do it.

"*Sanibonani*," he raised his hand in greeting as he neared them. Only one boy turned to stare at him.

"*Ufunani*? What do you want?"

"My friend's car is stuck in a hole. Will you help us get it out?"

A second youth turned to face him. "How much will you give us?" The youth moved in front of his friends but not before Simeon saw that they were scratching through a leather wallet. Scraps of paper floated to their feet. Like vultures around a kill, the youths pecked at the wallet for the spoil.

"I have no money." Simeon stepped back. Careful and slow. "Perhaps my friend will give you some."

By this time, all five youth stared at him. The short one holding the wallet slipped it into his pocket. He drew himself to his tallest height, "We cannot help you without money."

"I have nothing."

The short youth raised eyebrows to his friends which started a short, animated discussion. The youth nodded and stepped forward. His arm snapped out to the boy on his right. Into his open palm the other boy slapped a length of lead piping.

Simeon stiffened. He slowly took another step back.

But, like a leopard with its eyes on the prey, the short boy had Simeon in his sights.

Simeon's brain cried "run" but his legs didn't hear and locked in place. Instead, he reached into his back pocket and pulled out his wallet with trembling fingers. "I have R11." Sensing the almost physical vibrations of rampant violence in front of him, he stared at the pipe now raised inches from his head.

"You tell us you have no money." The youth stepped up nose to nose with Simeon.

"It is my bus money to get home from work today."

Too late. Simeon saw the lead pipe come down. He raised his arm to protect his head and the pipe drove into his wrist. He heard the bones shatter. He crumpled to the ground, the damaged wrist dangling at his side. The second blow missed his head again and in Simeon's pain-crazed mind he lost count of the times it connected with other parts of his body.

The other boys joined in. Shoes battered his chest and head. Fists pummeled his screaming body. Simeon could feel himself giving in. His mind cried out for them to stop but the words never made it to his mouth.

A sudden lull in the storm of blows came with a shrill cry from one of the boys. The battering slowed then stopped. Simeon lay still. Listening. When nothing more happened he tried to lift his head off the red earth. It wouldn't budge. Maybe he could move it sideways, but he couldn't see. Willing his eyes to open with all that was left of his strength, his left eye finally opened enough to see daylight, but within seconds the fine thread of light disappeared into darkness. Someone had switched off the sun.

Why had his attackers stopped like that? He heard labored breathing and faint shuffling in the sand close to him. Finally the breathing faded into silence. They had gone.

He lay wondering what his next move should be and doubted he'd ever do anything again. Then, in the distance, he picked up the mournful sound of singing and the pounding and scuffle of many feet drawing closer. A funeral procession arriving. He tried to stand. The shock to his damaged body yelled at him to be still. He closed his eyes and waited.

After several minutes Simeon realized two things. There was no change in the rhythm and noise of the mourners. They hadn't noticed him. Secondly, he was not going anywhere without help.

He tried again. Searing pain slashed through his body. Just a few minutes, then he'd try once more. He became aware of the cool earth under him and his body began to shake. No, not now. Tremors shook his broken body, sending it into screaming tension. He tried to relax but the shaking intensified. Then mercifully, a great tiredness overcame him and swallowed him whole. He disappeared into blackness.

Unaware of how long he'd be lying there, he eased back into consciousness as damaged nerves sent out deputies of pain to every corner of his body. For several long seconds his mind searched for the reason he was here. He remembered. How long had he been here? He listened. He could hear a man speaking, interjected by the crowd's heartfelt response. Thank God. They were still there. He had to get their attention.

But his mind strayed. Why was it so cold? What time was it? He had to get back to Mrs. Morgan. He opened his mouth to shout. His engorged lips could only open enough to let an ant in. It hurt. Everything hurt. He couldn't move. He couldn't see. The only thing he could do was feel, and he wished with all his heart he couldn't.

He forced himself to focus. If he didn't do something soon, the people would go and he would be left alone.

The man's voice finally stopped and for a few seconds the crowd was quiet. How could he draw attention to himself? His right hand dangled from his smashed wrist. His left elbow screamed to be left alone. Spasms of pain shot up his leg and into his hip when he tried to move them.

He began to panic. He summoned the last of his resources to raise his marginally less-painful left arm. It fluttered six inches off the ground then slapped down again onto the ground, landing on something hard. A stick. Thank God. Willing himself to focus, he teased the stick under his hand until he was able to hold it so that it rested on the 'v' between his thumb and index finger. He folded his fingers around the stick, raised it and waved it slowly from side to side praying that someone would see him. His hand thudded back onto the ground and he knew no more.

CHAPTER 7

Moses and Samson shrank away from Ida as she tried to read their faces.

"Who will kill you if you tell me?"

Moses edged sideways out of Ida's reach. Her eyes were unblinking and enormous in the dying light of the fire, her hands were on the ground behind her propping her up, and her feet were ready for flight.

Ida stepped back from them and straightened. "It's okay. It's okay." Soft and slow. She inched backward until she observed a slight loosening in their taut bodies. "I won't let anyone hurt you."

Samson muttered something which Ida strained to hear.

"Say that again," she said.

"You cannot help us when you go home." He snatched a look at Ida then dropped his head between his knees.

"I want to help you."

Samson began to rise. "No one can help us."

Ida watched the child shamble into his home. "You don't have to tell me if you don't want to," she called after his retreating back. "I just want to be your friend." He re-emerged a few seconds later, holding the stump of a candle hot-waxed to the bottom of a saucer. Around the edge of the fire he searched for and found a piece of dry grass which he thrust into the last burning embers. When the grass burst into flame he lit his candle, flicked the grass onto the ash and disappeared inside his house.

Getting the children to talk was going to be like persuading a cat stranded in a thorn tree to jump into your arms.

One by one the children drifted off to bed. Only Moses and Ida remained, staring into ashes. In the light of the moon, Moses' bowed head cast deep shadows across her face.

"Are you sad?" Ida's fingers stroked the thin shoulders.

She nodded.

"Are you afraid?"

A few moments and Ida saw a slight dip of the head. She waited before continuing.

"Is someone hurting you?"

Moses turned her face away. No response.

Ida waited but Moses was done.

"Why don't we go to bed?" Ida rose, eased her hand into the child's and pulled her up. "Where shall I sleep tonight?"

Moses led her to her house, past the two boys sprawled across the mattress asleep, and into a second room the same size as the first. An uncovered window let in enough moonlight to reveal a two-seater couch whose worn cushions sagged in the middle. It stood next to a small formica table. Pushed into the table were two mismatched plastic chairs.

Ida wondered where they kept all their "things". Perhaps they were under that pile of stuff, covered by the grubby tablecloth next to the window.

Moses pointed to the couch.

Ida tried to visualize the two of them sleeping on the two-seater. It would be easier to sleep sitting up. She looked up as Moses moved off. "Where are you going?" She followed Moses into the boys' room. It took a little while for her eyes to adjust to the dimness.

She saw the shape of Moses push Surprise into the center of the sheetless mattress next to the dark form of Bandile. Moses then picked up the thin blanket and flicked it over her brothers' bodies. Still holding a corner of the blanket she jumped in next to Surprise and pulled it over her legs.

Ida spoke softly into the shadows, "Goodnight, Moses." She stepped outside, aware of the padding of her feet as she walked over to the house of Samson and Phineas. The door hinges screeched as she tried to open it, so she left it and crept around to the window, stepping aside to let in the moonlight. The boys lay on a coarse grey blanket on the concrete floor. The corners of the blanket covered Phineas' legs. Samson lay on his back with his arms out-flung, his left hand resting on his brother's head. The room was empty of furniture except for a large drum on the opposite corner of the room.

Ida leaned against the outside wall of the house. For two years she'd been feeling sorry for herself. Sure, she had a right to mourn and be angry, but behind those walls were two little boys whose only possessions were each other and a drum. The churning deep down in her soul intensified until she could no longer keep it in.

She flew as far as she could away from the houses and howled into the night–a gushing stream of pain and sadness. Belonging to no one, these children were discarded diamonds in the dust:

undiscovered, uncut, unpolished; fit only to be ignored or stamped upon. For goodness' sake, even garbage could be recycled and become useful again.

When she'd emptied her soul, she stared up at the stars. Brilliant specks of light sprayed across the inky blackness. Maybe one day, these little gems would shine too.

She took her questions and her emptiness to bed. Before entering Moses' house, she picked up the two cooking pots from the fire pit and a thick, stripped branch which she'd been keeping her eye on all afternoon. They would have to do. After closing the door she picked up a plastic chair and jammed it against the door. Onto the chair she placed the pots. If anyone came in at least she would have some warning. The stick lay next to her on the couch.

Even without having to share the lumpy couch with Moses, Ida couldn't get comfortable. Every time she moved, swirls of dust clogged her throat. At first the lingering warmth of the day kept her warm, but within a couple of hours the temperature cooled to a point where she had to hug herself to keep warm. She searched around for a piece of fabric–anything to keep her warm and protect her from the persistent mosquitoes. There was nothing but the tablecloth over there. You never knew what might be hiding in that lot. She'd do without.

Then she noticed the corner of a newspaper sticking out from the bottom of the pile under the tablecloth. Pinching the end of it between her thumb and forefinger she teased it out. At the window, she thrust it through the opening and shook it out to relieve it of any unwelcome creatures. She turned her face away as a cloud of dust spewed out. A careful inspection revealed a spider's web sticking two pages together. Satisfied the web was abandoned she broke its hold and tried to read the date on the front page. If she wasn't mistaken it said, "September 16, 1999". Printed before Bandile was even thought of.

She lay back on the couch. It was strange how the crackling of the newspaper as she covered herself sounded so loud in the darkness. Pity it didn't reduce the repetitive thump of distant drums. Someone out there was summoning up his ancestors.

*

The chatter of birds and dawn's first light wakened Ida. She was surprised to realize she had finally gone to sleep. She guessed it was about five-thirty. So, no *panga*-wielding hordes had come by.

Stretching cramped legs over the end of the couch, she groaned, waiting for the pain and numbness to ease. She rubbed her cool arms, wincing at the red welts of mosquito bites. The temptation to scratch was overwhelming. Instead, she ran her fingers through her hair. The grit between her teeth crunched when she bought her teeth together. A tissue would do. She reached into her bag for one to rub off the worst of the night's film. What she wouldn't do for a steaming cup of tea, a hot bath, and a toothbrush.

She tiptoed to the door, removed the pots and chair and stepped into the brisk morning air. The air felt vacuumed and cleaned and then chilled to an invigorating temperature. She breathed deeply the sweet smell of an African morning, longing for it to linger for more than just a moment. Through the grasses a breeze whispered promises of peace.

The squeak of the door and the shuffle of feet broke the morning's magic. Moses hurried up to her. She grabbed Ida's hand and dragged her to her house. Surprise lay on his back, eyes closed, squirming from side to side.

Ida dropped onto the bed. She placed her hand on his forehead. "He's on fire." She jumped up. "Moses, we need the rest of the water. And a cloth–and a cup." Moses rushed out and came back with Promise's water container in one hand and an ancient towel and a mug in the other.

"Surprise, we're going to try and make you feel better." Ida whispered in his ear then filled the cup with water, placing it on the floor next to her. She lifted his head and placed the mug to his lips. He drank noisily. Next she sprinkled water on the end of the towel. "Moses please find out if Samson is up yet. Ask him to run to the river and get some water, please."

Surprise mumbled and tried to shove aside the cool wet cloth on his body. With gentle but firm hands Ida replaced the cloth. "I know it's not nice but it will make you feel better." He began to shiver and tried to curl up to keep warm.

Next to the sick child, Bandile stirred. Ida looked at him. "Surprise is sick," she said.

The older boy bent over his brother and shook him, "Wake up.

Wake up." When Surprise did not respond he reached over and gripped him in a fierce hug. Ida saw the panic in his eyes, "He will be okay," she said softly. "But we need some water for him. Will you go with Samson to get some?"

Half an hour went by. The boys had not come back. Promise entered the room and sat next to Ida on the bed.

"Why are the boys taking so long?" Ida held the towel up. It was almost dry and Surprise was still hot.

"It is a long way to the river and the bucket is heavy."

What did she expect?

When Ida saw that Surprise was asleep she slipped outside behind the house. Her gaze followed the path that led down to the river. At last, from around a bend the boys became visible, both holding the bucket. Even from where she was, Ida could see the water sloshing over the edge as the children plodded along under its weight.

She hurried down to them. "Let me help you."

The boys let go, shaking arms and flattened fingers.

"Thank you," she said. Within a few seconds she knew she was in trouble, too. The combination of a solid tin bucket and the weight of the water were too heavy for her. She stopped and poured some water out. "How did you boys manage to walk so far?"

Samson ran onto the path ahead of her and turned round so that he walked backward. "*Mama*, we heard some women talking at the river. They said it is bad at the road. There is fighting and the people they are throwing stones at the cars."

Not good. There was no way they'd get past the altercation at the road safely. They couldn't go that way. "How am I going to get Surprise to a doctor?" Ida said between puffs.

"You can walk." Bandile spoke up from behind her.

"But it is too far."

"If you go with the river it not so far."

Of course. The children had followed Moses–right to her house. For the first time since she'd arrived, Ida felt a spark of hope. If the children could do it, she could, too. Except for one thing: Surprise. She'd never be able to carry him that far. She had to make a plan.

After sponging Surprise down with river water and seeing him comfortable, Ida called the children together. "I want you all to come home with me until I can find a way to help you."

Zinhle giggled. Promise nudged her and frowned. The little girl pressed her hands together, trying not to smile.

Standing next to Moses, Sampson whispered, "God has ears." For several seconds Ida wrestled with his words. Tucking them into her memory, she continued.

"We have some problems." She looked at each child in front of her. "We have no car. Simeon has not come back and Surprise is sick."

After explaining her idea she asked, "Does anyone want to come home with me?" Seven hands shot up. "We will wait one more hour in case Simeon comes. Then we must go."

While the younger children scattered to get firewood to boil water for the journey Ida spoke to Moses and Samson.

"Moses, would you put the fruit in a bag? Then give the children the rest of the food I brought." As the child ran off Ida called after her, "See if you can get Surprise to eat a banana." She then turned to Samson. "How many matches do you have left?"

He held up two fingers.

She held him by the shoulders. "Be very careful when you light the fire. We need clean water."

She snatched up her bag and started up the hill. Arriving at the car, she saw nothing appeared to have been stolen and the tires were intact. She scanned the contents of the trunk. Lots of junk, but there was Tony's golf bag and Wilson's clubs that she was planning to take to the second-hand store. She studied them to see which ones would be most effective then lifted out the three and five irons and laid them on the brown earth. Sorry, Tony. She needed them to carry Surprise.

Next she reached in behind the clubs and hauled out her grocery cart, its wheels neatly folded under it. The empty water bottle might come in handy, too. Rummaging around, she found the gardening shears she was going to have sharpened, a tangled length of twine, and a piece of hessian. She placed them next to the golf clubs.

Perhaps there was something inside the car she could use, too. A surge of hot air hit her as she opened the door. So early in the morning. Avoiding contact with the scorching, navy blue interior, she glanced inside. Nothing.

She had just taken the key out the lock when a figure came

running down the path. His head flicked round now and then to look behind him.

As he grew closer, Ida saw that his shirt was torn at his shoulder and a thin stream of blood coursed down his forehead into his right eye. He noticed Ida and raced up to her, "Can you take me in your car?" he asked, between gasps of air.

"What did you do?" Ida said, ready to run or defend herself.

"Some boys want me to drink with them, but they are throwing rocks at cars. When I say no, they hit me."

Ida looked into the grave face and believed him. "My car is stuck. I'm sorry."

"It is fine." He attempted a smile. "But *Mama*, you cannot stay here. They are looking for a fight." He fled down the hill followed by Ida dragging the clattering cart behind her. The golf clubs needed to be held in position and slowed her down. Halfway down, she snatched a look up the hill where three figures crested the summit. She looked down to see how far the young man had got. He had disappeared. She hurried on.

CHAPTER 8

Drawing level with the houses, she stole another quick look up the hill. The three youths circled her car, peering into it. Anger welled up in her throat. That car was her only means of getting around. If they…

No time. She was no match for three angry, drunk youths. The car might actually distract them for a while. They had to get going. "Moses. Samson. Everyone. Come quickly," she shouted.

All seven children scurried before her. "We need to go. Now. Samson, is the water ready?" He lifted up the water container and a mug. "Moses, show me how to wrap Surprise on my back like your mother used to do." She and the girl dashed into the house. Over her shoulder, Ida called to Bandile. "Throw those golf clubs–those sticks–in the bushes over there. And those other things. " She indicated the string and hessian. Forget trying to make a stretcher. She'd have to come back for them another time.

Ida called the children together. "You may take one thing with you that is important to you," she said. "Something small."

They all rushed over to their houses. Phineas came out first, staggering under the weight of the drum Ida had seen in the boy's room.

"Phineas." How could she tell him? It was the only thing the boys possessed. She dropped onto her haunches and faced him. "We have a long way to walk today. You are a big boy but this drum is too heavy for you."

"Samson he can carry it for me." He clutched it tighter to him.

"I am so sorry, Phineas. We cannot take it."

"I can pull it on the sheet." He stared at her, eyes wide.

Ida shook her head gently.

The boy's eyes filled. "It is my father's drum. He make it."

"I make you a promise, Phineas. I will come back to get it when I get my car." She felt like a lion eating a mother springbok while its baby looked on. "Put it back in your house so I will know where to find it when I come." She nudged him in the direction of his house. His chin fell to his chest but he stumbled back into his house with the drum. She followed a few meters behind him. He gently lowered the drum in the corner of the room, dragged the sheet over it and tucked his precious instrument in the corner.

"Good thinking," Ida said from the doorway. "That will keep the dust off until I come back for it. Is there anything else you want to take?" Then added, "That's small." He walked outside to the fire pit and searched a small area around it. Every now and then he picked up something off the ground, rubbed the sand off it and put it in his pocket. The realization dawned on Ida. It was food. Tiny blobs of pap that had dropped from hungry hands last night. The muscles round her heart tightened. How hungry do you have to be to eat food off the ground? There was no vacation, no break from the challenges these children faced.

Promise returned with a well worn exercise book and the stub of a pencil. Behind her Zinhle held little Agnus' hand. Ida stepped closer to see which treasure the younger child had chosen. Zinhle opened her sister's palm to reveal a sliver of soap. She raised it to Ida's nose.

Ida bent over, closed her eyes and breathed in deeply. "Ah." She said trying in vain to distinguish the soap's faded fragrance.

The child smiled and slipped the soap into the pocket of her dress.

"What about you, Zinhle?"

From out of a pocket in her skirt, Zinhle lifted up a huge pair of tortoise-shell glasses. The lens for the right eye was missing. She lifted them onto her nose and squinted through them at Ida. "They is for sewing for my *Mama*."

Ida hugged the sisters and looked up to see Bandile standing behind them. A round bulge in his pocket said he carried a ball.

Within a minute all the children stood before Ida. But someone was missing.

"Samson?" When there was no reply, Ida hurried over to his house.

The boy sat in the middle of the blanket staring at the bare room. Ida waited as long as she dared. Then, "We need to go."

He turned away from her.

"What's wrong?" She walked around him to look into his eyes.

"I do not want to go."

Had she heard correctly? "But there is nothing here for you."

"My mother she was here."

"Samson, I cannot leave you here by yourself."

"When my uncle come and take all our things, he say he will come back for Phineas and me."

"When did your uncle come?"

"When my mother die."

"How old were you when your mother died?"

"I am five."

"So your uncle came about four years ago?"

He shrugged.

"You have waited a long time."

He remained quiet.

Ida decided to change tack. "What about the men? You said they will hurt you?"

"If am alone, I can hide. They cannot find me."

"Please, Samson. I want to help you." Ida snatched a look at her watch. "If you come with me I will help you look for your uncle."

He shook his head. "My mother she live here."

Now what? Short of tying him up, she couldn't make him come. She kneeled in front of him. "Please, Samson."

He stood to his feet and backed away from Ida.

"I cannot wait anymore." As Ida hugged him she felt him pulling away from her. "I will come back and see how you are." Taking a step into the sunshine, she said, "Come and say goodbye to Phineas." She held out her hand to him.

As they approached the children she dropped his hand. He moved over to his little brother and said something she couldn't hear. Phineas started to cry.

Samson patted his brother's back. "When Uncle come we will get you." He studied the other children briefly then wandered back into his house without looking back and shut the door.

Ida stared at the door the boy had closed. Samson, you won't have to wait for me for four years. I will be back. Soon.

It was a subdued group Promise led down the path to the river. Midway through the line of children, Ida carried Surprise on her back, bound tightly with the table cloth. She found herself leaning forward a little to take the weight of the child off her spine.

Directly behind her, Bandile tossed the ball. Only its size and shape suggested it was a tennis ball. It didn't matter to him that his ball had exceeded its projected life span by a few hundred years. Every now and then he stopped tossing it to pick at the few tufts of soiled yellow fluff that still clung to the dark grey rubber sphere.

Bringing up the rear was Moses, pulling the grocery cart with the water and food. Her face gave away nothing. Ida could see neither hope nor fear, just a blank canvas.

The last time Ida had checked on the three youths they were at the driver's side of her car but too far away to see what they were doing. Now they were no longer visible as the path descended sharply down a section of rocky outcrops.

The extra weight on her back made it difficult for Ida to pick her way over the rocks, slippery with sand and dry vegetation. Unprotected by the shade of trees and shrubs, the sun's glare seared her eyes. Good thing it was still early.

For another twenty meters they descended until the terrain flattened out into a valley through which a stream of clear water flowed over smooth, flat rocks. Some twenty meters on either side of the stream tall grass, scattered trees, and brush grew.

A lone woman bending over to fill her bucket straightened and tightened her long wraparound skirt. She stared at the large group. "*Sanibonani,*" she said. "*Kunjani?* How are you?"

"*Sawubona, Mama.*" Ida finished the greeting and spoke to the children. "Let's have some water under the tree. Then we must go."

Relieved to have Surprise off her back for a short while, she lowered him onto the tablecloth spread at her feet. She felt his head. Still hot.

A sudden crunch of dry twigs behind her sent her heartbeat racing. She swung round. A little girl of about four rushed past her, limping. She made for a spot in the stream where the water whirlpooled round a circular rock formation. At the edge of it, a stretch of sand made a convenient place to stop and collect water. When she reached the water's edge she whipped off the large plastic bowl she carried on her head and knelt down. Then, scooping the bowl into the stream, she hauled up a half bowl of water and dragged it onto the sand. She looked back along the path she'd come.

"*Sheshisa.* Hurry up," A woman came into view along the same path as the child.

The child's head dropped down. Stretching her arms around the basin, she tried to stand up from a crouching position. Her foot slipped under her and she fell, the water cascading over her shapeless grey dress. She gasped as the cool water drenched her.

"You are no good to me." The woman stormed up to the child and yanked her up by her arm. With her free hand she snatched up the basin. "You are too small. You cannot work for me." As she let the child go, the child tried to find her footing and once more her foot buckled under her and sent her sprawling into the shallows.

The child crawled back to the woman and pulled at her skirt. "*Mama*, I can do it."

The woman shrugged her off and filled the bowl. "Do not come back to my house. When you are big I will see."

The woman with the wraparound skirt heaved a full bucket onto her head. "*Unga khulumi kanjalo*. Don't talk like that. Give her a smaller bucket."

"It is not your business." The second woman raised the basin onto her head and set off, each step planted firmly to the rhythm of her body with not a drip from the basin.

The child watched the woman's retreating back like a hungry pup having its food snatched away. When she could no longer see the woman she slumped onto the sand and drew her fingers through its moist granules.

The first woman called to her, "*Mtwana,* child, what is your name?"

An empty face stared up at her. "Goodness," she said. She went back to her drawing.

"Where are your parents?" the woman asked.

"My mother she is dead. I have no father." She picked up a small stick and poked it in the sand.

"Who looks after you?"

She shook her head and shrugged.

"You are alone?"

The little eyebrows rose with an imperceptible tilt of the head.

Ida moved over to the woman. "*Mama*, why does that woman not take the child into her house?"

"Maybe she is too poor."

To her right, the child stopped jabbing the sand. "She does not want my mother's spirit in her house."

Ida sighed and crossed over to the child. "Goodness, would you like to come to my house with these children? I will help you. You will not have to work for your food."

The child studied Ida's face. Ida smiled and reached for her hand. The child took it and rose to her feet.

"Let me see your foot." Ida raised the small foot so that it rested on her leg. In the middle of the child's arch she saw a swelling with two tiny pinpricks in the centre. Spider bite. It was going to be uncomfortable for her to walk for a while. After leading the child to the stream to clean the bite, she scratched around in her bag and found a single band aid. That should protect it from the dirt. For now.

"Time to go, everyone," she called to the children. Surprise lay watching her with half-open eyes. She called to Moses, "Please help me with Surprise. We must go." Between her and Moses, they attached Surprise to her back.

Just then shouts came from the direction they'd traveled. Ida grew rigid. If she wasn't mistaken, the three youths had arrived.

CHAPTER 9

The man swung his VW Beetle onto his short dirt driveway. The car dipped and dived as he negotiated the rain-eroded earth, swinging him from side to side until it jerked to a stop in front of his grey-brick house.

Good thing the wife wasn't home yet. He had some phoning to do before the nagging started. He glanced over at Mrs. Ncube next door hanging her washing on the wire mesh fence. She stopped and stared at him. He opened the car door and peeled out, grabbing his jacket and bag from the back seat.

"*Kunjani?*" he said, not waiting for a reply. He knew he was being rude but the whole world knew everyone's secrets the moment she opened her mouth. The less she knew about his, the better. Keeping his head down, he hurried to the front door. He groped for his key, while clutching his belongings.

Once inside, he looked at his watch. He relaxed a little when he realized it was a good hour before his wife walked home from the bus stop. He hurled his belongings onto the red two-seater couch that he was still paying the interest for after two years. He found a cold beer in the almost empty fridge, flung open the window, and lowered himself into the single armchair facing the window. As the frosty liquid eased down his parched throat, his body melted into the chair. His legs flopped out in front of him.

Through the window, a cool breeze teased the surface of his face. He closed his eyes and lifted his face to the wind. Slowly the peace of the moment enticed him into sleep.

A sudden noise jolted him awake; the sound of his wife's jagged voice greeting Mrs. Ncube next door. Outside the window, the sun had already moved behind Legogote Mountain. He must have slept away the hour.

He stumbled out of the chair, snatched up his jacket and crept out the back door, closing it silently behind him. Keeping his head down, he disappeared behind the banana trees in the small back garden. His fingers scrabbled through his jacket pockets. Where was the stupid phone? Finally he found it in the inside pocket. With trembling fingers he dialed the number. He peered between the giant banana leaves to see if his wife had spotted him. No sign of her yet.

"*Sawubona. Kunjani?*" His voice quiet, behind cupped hands.

His gaze strayed constantly to the house.

"We go at full moon." His eyes narrowed as he listened. "It has to be. There is no electricity there. Yes, that is three days' time. Friday." After a little haggling, they settled on a figure he was happy with. Ecstatic actually. It was double a month's wages. He had a thought. "I can't take more than three men." He strained to see through the mountain of untidy foliage. "I have a small car."

"Where are you?" The complaint shot like a cannon from the kitchen, interrupting his thoughts. He could hear his wife muttering to herself. "A *shongololo* has more brains in its many little feet than this man."

When he did not respond he heard the groan of the kitchen door on its dry hinges and footsteps tread lightly across the hard packed, swept earth. He slipped further round the banana tree making himself as thin as possible. He folded his phone and tucked it into his back pocket.

"*Eeish*! Why you hiding behind the banana trees? Were you looking for your monkey friends?" She stood in front of him, arms barely crossing over abundant mounds of flesh.

The man grew hot on the inside. It was easier to stop a dam bursting than this. He waited for the scorching lava of hate to cool down. One day she would take a step too close to his manhood. Then he would do what he had wanted to since the day after he married her. And he would smile as he did it.

Instead, he lifted his chin and stared into the distance. "Oh," he said, "it is cool in the shade." He sauntered toward the house, feeling the barrage of her words but deflecting their aim so that none penetrated. She pursued close behind. He pictured her arms pummeling the air in a dramatic show of unrighteous indignation and blasting the air with battery-acid spite.

As he passed through the house he snatched up his now warm and flat beer and marched out into the front garden. It was getting harder and harder to squelch the anger that threatened to detonate inside him. He could feel it now, beginning to erode the delicate lining of his sanity.

Sitting on the cool concrete step below his front door, he focused down the dirt track waiting for the boys to come home. They would deflect her attention so he could breathe freely again.

At last the boys appeared around the corner. With arms outstretched to balance, they placed one foot in front of each other along the ridges of deep ruts on the trail. The man watched as every now and then one would push the other to unseat his rival from his balancing act. They didn't see him there.

He had done that, too. A lifetime ago. Forbidden thoughts surged to the surface of his mind. How many times had he walked home as a boy–alone? And wondering what waited for him when he opened the door to the shack he shared with his mother and two sisters? His mother sprawled on the only bed, an old towel covering her head. From under it–wrenching sobs. Bending down to wrap his arm around her and being thrust away with an angry, "Get away from me. It's all your fault."

An iron pot whistling past his head, accompanied by a curse. Or, "Go away, you useless piece of rubbish. You were supposed to die before you were born."

Every day was different. Today, silence. Tomorrow, unstoppable words of condemnation. The next day, a piece of fresh bread appeasing yesterday's harsh realities.

Sometimes, it was the beating stick, then escaping to the river and creeping home when he could hear her snores. Of all his memories, the beatings were the easiest to smother. The aches and pain were physical. It was the words that wounded with deadly force and rendered yet another small piece of him withered or dead.

He was ten when he finally buried his emotional needs, in a dark hole in his mind, and he never searched for them again. Sitting there watching his son and nephew approach him, almost forgotten scenes of that last night shone on the screen of his memory.

He lay on his corner of the communal bed pretending to sleep. His fingers crept up to his ears to stop the sounds of insanity. A man— not his father—stepped through the door: the beginning of the end of life as he knew it. When he finally opened his eyes his mother lay dead on the floor and his sisters were gone.

On that night, the last remaining residue of human warmth hardened into quick-drying concrete in his heart. He ran away. It was a good thing, not feeling. It protected you. It made you feel strong and in control.

He didn't remember much of that night. He'd run so fast, for so long, that even today, 30 years later, he had no idea where his mother's house used to be.

When exhaustion finally caught up with him he sank onto the earth, next to a small building of wooden planks hammered together. He sat there pressed against the wall, legs drawn up, conscious of the hammering of his heart and he knew it wasn't the pumping of his blood that sent waves of nausea into his mouth. He searched through the darkness while the moon rose in the sky. But no one chased him. Nothing moved. The panic subsided.

Maybe this building was empty. By the moon's light he could see it had no windows. Maybe it was a church. At first he sat on the sand listening to the sounds of the night. The ever-blaring radios were silent now. A dog barked. The world around him sank into silence. He tried the door. It opened. Beams of moonlight filtered through the lattice work of planks above his head. Scattered around the room, sat benches of all sizes and conditions. On the floor, irregular pieces of end-carpet covered parts of the floor.

He knew after the rain, the pressure of many feet had stomped the carpet into the mud. Now the mud was dry and if he tipped the benches over and lay them on their sides he could surround himself with benches and have a sense of safety. He chose the largest piece of carpet and lay down.

He stiffened. Voices approaching. He curled up silently and made himself as small as he could. Almost stopped breathing. He waited. The voices passed by.

"*Sawubona, Baba.*" The voice of his son shattered his reverie. The man jumped up, disoriented. He looked around him, his heart pounding. He'd all but disappeared into the past. The pounding turned to pain for the first time in all these years. With all the strength he could summon, he bore down on the tears that threatened to undo his control. He fled for the bushes growing up the mountainside behind his house, unaware of his son calling, "*Baba? Baba?*"

CHAPTER 10

Simeon eased into consciousness with a rising crescendo of pain. Where was he? He felt the throb behind his eyes which only intensified when he tried to open them. He gave that up. He knew he lay on a very narrow bed in some kind of room.

Around him, he heard the ebb and flow of indistinct conversations. Disjointed, disconnected speech. The odd spurt of laughter then moments of silence. Clattering pans. Whirring rubber wheels moving along a smooth surface.

Snatches of words reached him: "Take Mrs. Sifunda…to 6a."

Two plus two was beginning to add up to four. He was in hospital. Must be Themba Hospital.

No one spoke to him. No one came near. As he opened his mouth, his lips peeled open. So sore. "Water," he said, but even his own ears couldn't hear it above a whisper. For the first time he thought he was going to die and that no one would even notice. "Water." This came out a little louder. Encouraged, he tried again. At last, footsteps moved in his direction and stopped at his side.

"What is it?" a female voice answered.

"Water."

"You cannot drink until the doctor has seen you," she said.

He felt a tear escape his bulging eyelid and stung as it trickled down his damaged face onto the bed. He didn't care who saw it. His throat grew thick. "Please."

The footsteps receded and returned a short while later. A hand reached under his head, "Just a little bit." He sucked in the water, unconcerned for the tributaries of liquid tumbling out the corners of his mouth.

"How long have I been here?" he asked the voice when the water was finished.

"A few hours," the voice answered above his head. "You are lucky. A man brought you in his car. He was at the funeral and he saw you lying on the ground."

Simeon was thoughtful. "Did he tell you his name?"

No one answered.

"Nurse?"

She was no longer there.

The night dragged by. He knew from past experience how long it took to get attended to. How often had he sat here with his mother? Waiting, if they were lucky, on a hard wooden bench. He would put his young arms around her fragile body and help her to the washroom. He would leave her at the door, hoping some kind woman would help her once she was inside the "Ladies". Men weren't allowed in there, so he had to wait outside. When she finally came out, he could see her little trip to the washroom had cost her.

Each time they'd come, she returned home in the taxi bus with a little less spark. Then she wasn't strong enough to go to the hospital anymore and the spark went out altogether.

How he missed her. She should have been here. She should be talking to him and telling him he was going to be alright like when he was little. She would bring him some water and talk kindly to him.

If only he could sleep away the pain. If he could just find a comfortable position on this hard bed. Random thoughts flittered around his head, searching for a quiet place to rest but never finding it as he slipped in and out of troubled sleep.

Finally, silent hands grabbed his bed and he felt himself being wheeled away. He heard the rip of a curtain being pulled aside and the bed moved forward a little and then came to a stop.

Receding footsteps, then relative quiet. He dozed off, waking with a start when a man's voice said, "My, my, my. What kind of hyenas were you fighting off?" He felt the man's hands probe every hurting place on his body. "I am Doctor Mantlaka."

Between swollen lips, Simeon told his story. Every now and then he would stop his story to answer the doctor's questions.

"You are very lucky." The doctor's hands ran down his leg. As he reached the calf area, Simeon let out a yell. "You are young and strong. You will get better. Where are your parents?"

"I have no parents. I live with my *gogo*."

The doctor continued to probe, "I need to see what's going on here." Simeon turned his head away, trying not to scream. "You have a bad break in your tibia. And because your wrist has been shattered it will be a while before you can use your hand again."

Simeon fought to keep back the tears. Where would he get money if he couldn't work? *Gogo*'s small pension and smaller spaza shop were hardly enough to feed them both.

When the doctor had finished, Simeon could hear him beside the bed, breathing deeply. "We need to bring down the swelling in your eyes before we can see if there is any damage there. The nurse will put a cast on your wrist and leg when I am finished. I don't think there is anything broken in your back but I am concerned there has been kidney damage."

"Doctor, please could you help me? I need to phone the lady I work for. She is waiting for me."

"I have too many patients to see to. Tell the nurse when she comes in just now. She will help you."

Simeon waited until he heard footsteps near his bed. "Nurse?"

Silence. The footsteps faded away. Ten minutes later, more footsteps. Again he called. "Nurse?"

"I am busy. What do you want?"

"Please get my cell phone out my pocket." He felt hands move into his pockets.

"There's no cell phone," the nurse said.

"It must be there. Please try again."

"I have looked. There is no cell phone." The nurse moved away and left Simeon feeling more alone than he'd ever felt in his life.

He had made Mrs. Morgan go to Masoyi when she was so afraid and he promised he would help her. Now he couldn't even get off the bed to look for his cell phone. More painful than his desperately hurting body was the knowledge he had let her down.

Another 30 minutes of waiting and his bed began to move again.

"What is happening?" he said. Why didn't anyone talk to him? "Where are you taking me?"

"I am taking you to theatre," a male voice said.

Simeon found the pulsating bounce of the gurney almost comforting as it rolled along hallways and swung round corners until it finally stopped. Within fifteen minutes, his mind shut down and all the pain stopped.

CHAPTER 11

Ida heard the voices first, calling to each other. Then, through the brush in front of her, burst a young man, clutching a Castle Lager in his right hand and shouting to someone behind him, "They are here."

He slid down the last of the embankment, snagged his foot on the protruding root of a weeping willow and sprawled onto the sand. The momentum sent his shoes rising swiftly to kick himself in the pants. As his head shot up, his gaze caught Ida eyeing his shoes where his feet showed through gaping holes in the soles. He spun round, quick to draw his feet under him, and was trying to get up when another youth came barreling through the bushes, tripped over him, and planted his face in the sand.

By the time a third youth appeared, a bottle raised to his mouth, the children were hanging onto each other, their shrieks of hilarity piercing the quietness of the bush.

The third youth saw too late the outstretched bodies of his friends in his path. To avoid landing on them, he extended his leg in a painful split, ramming his foot into the soft sand. He began to topple sideways, slow and steady. Unfortunately for him, the one hand available to steady him also gripped the bottle, the contents of which he was unwilling to part with just yet. The bottle smacked the earth with a thud. Up shot the beer in a spray of fizzle and froth right into his left ear. For a few seconds, all sound was sucked into stillness as the onlookers waited to see what would happen next.

When no one appeared terminally injured or threatening, Ida turned her attention to the children. Their wild hilarity resumed and stimulated in her gut an almost forgotten feeling. Bubbling up in a cauldron of mirth, laughter erupted from her, pouring out with it the tension of the moment. She fell next to the rolling children and let it all out.

It was short lived. A chance look at the teens abruptly shut her mouth and stemmed the flow of amusement.

The first youth, his T-shirt hanging loosely from his thin shoulders, stood up with great deliberation, spat sand, and rubbed it off his face with the back of his hand. He glared at the children, his face stretched and taut.

"You laugh at me?" he searched around until he saw a rock protruding from the river bank, next to the trunk of a mature weeping willow. He slashed at the rock with the bottle. Its base shattered, leaving him holding the jagged neck end. He advanced toward the children the bottle thrust before him.

Moses suddenly came to life. She raced past Bandile, slapping him to get his attention, then grabbed Surprise and lumbered off into the bushes grasping her little brother by the waist. One by one the rest of the children followed, their laughter turned to screams.

Ida became stone. An avalanche of insecurity and fear came charging down to bury her. She stood transfixed as the youth swung round to face her.

He said nothing. He inched toward her. She stared into the red eyes of malice and drink. He raised the bottle.

Behind her, Ida heard the crunch of sand and thought her heart would stop. A soft voice spoke into her ear.

"Take the children. I will talk to the boys." The woman with the wraparound skirt appeared next to her and pushed her toward the children. Ida stumbled away.

The woman faced the youth. "A great fighter does not waste his strength on small things. He fights the lion to prove his power," she said.

"What do you know? You are a woman?"

"I know great people have great thoughts. I think you want to be great. You cannot be great when you fight that which cannot fight back."

"She is right," the second youth said. "The lion that kills a cub is not great. He is afraid."

The first youth turned to him and shoved him in the chest. "What's the matter with you?" He faced the woman again and lowered his voice. "You are not a cub. I will kill you." With one bound he reached the woman, gripped her arm and thrust the broken bottle to her throat, "But first we will see how great you are."

His two friends snickered and leaped to his side. The woman shrieked and pulled away from the sharp edge of the bottle. Her foot shot out landing on the first youth's hip, propelling him away from her. The other two youths grabbed her arms yanking them behind her back. Her legs shot out kicking indiscriminately at whatever flesh was closest. Finally, she twisted away and broke free but the sudden release of their hands drove her forward and she lost her footing. All three youths pounced on her and the beating began.

"Let her go." Ida stood squarely in front of them, holding a solid length of driftwood as long and thick as a walking stick. No more fear. She was ready to kill.

The first youth paused to stare at her. He held up a hand in warning to his friends. "*Yima*. Stop." Not hearing, they continued to kick the woman. "*Yima!*" he raised his voice.

Ida gripped the stick with both hands. "Stop now or I will beat you."

Suddenly from the bush behind the youth, a young voice yelled. "*Inyoka*. Snake."

The youths swung around to see who had spoken but no one was visible. "It is one of the children playing a trick."

Ida sneaked a look at the children behind her. A quick count showed them all there huddled together ready for flight, on the other side of the river. It wasn't any of them. "No, they're all there. Oh…," her hand flew to her throat, her other hand pointed to the weeping willow. "Over there…black mamba," she shouted and took a step backward, her eyes wide. "I don't play with snakes. You can have him." She turned, transferred the stick to her other hand and raced after the children. When she looked back the youths were disappearing up the river bank and around a bend.

Then Ida saw the woman. "Oh no." The woman scrabbled through the sand to drag herself away from the snake. Every few seconds she stopped to stare through paper-thin gaps betweens her swollen eyelids to search for the reptile. With each breath came a wail of fear. Ida flew over the sand and dropped to the woman's side. She threw her arms around her.

"There is no snake," Ida said as loudly as she dared above the noise of the woman's wails. The youths could possibly still be in the area. "There is no snake." The woman tried to look around Ida. Ida drew her closer. Finally she crumpled at Ida's feet, trembling; her body, cold.

A rustle in the bushes sent a new wave of panic through Ida.

"*Mama! Mama!*" a young voice said.

"Samson, it was you."

The boy scampered down from his hiding place in bushes above them and ran up to her. Ida rose and encircled the thin boy with her arms. No words, only the pressure of her hug telling the child he'd done well.

The woman began to moan. Ida returned to the woman and rocked her. The sobbing subsided and the woman grew quiet. Ida eased the woman's arms away from her face. Her left eye was one bulging eyelid. And the right one, only red showed through the thin line of exposed eye.

"Is anything broken?" Ida asked. She held onto the woman's good arm and helped her rise. The woman turned her head away from Ida as she tried to stand on her right leg. She cried out. She needed help to walk.

"How long to get to your house?" Ida asked.

"Maybe fifteen minutes."

Make that half an hour or more with her injuries. With the return journey, Ida was looking at least three quarters of an hour. Ida looked from the children to the woman. She turned to the woman who sat holding her head and staring at her. "How can I thank you for what you did?"

"When you help the children you help us. God bless you."

"*Mama*, I have a problem. I want to help you but I have all these children to look after, and one of them is very sick and needs a doctor."

"It is okay. My daughter will help me."

"Where do you live?" she asked the woman.

The woman pointed to the east side of the valley where the children lived, where the ground rose sharply up a steep hill.

Ida resisted the temptation to look at her watch. "Moses," she called, "I need to help the *mama* to her house. Take the children under a big tree. Somewhere safe. I don't think the boys will be back but be careful just in case. Wait for me there." Moses nodded, rounded up the children and led them into dense brush, a little distance away from the river.

Ida set off, bearing the weight of the woman who was easily half a head taller than she was and well covered. Together they struggled along the path that led up the eastern slope of the hill. They had been traveling some ten minutes when the woman stopped and stared up at a group of pole-and-*daga* huts halfway up the hill.

"Maria? *Buya*. Come." Her voice carried over the distance. Together they stood and watched. When no one appeared she called again.

Ida held her breath.

Then a youthful face appeared from around the corner of the hut holding a faded yellow, plastic bucket.

"*Mama?*" the young woman peered down at them. She dropped the bucket and ran down to meet them. "*Mama*, what happened?"

With wild gesticulations and shrill voice, the woman told her daughter.

"I am so sorry I cannot help you," Ida interrupted after the story had been told in a variety of ways. "I need to get the little boy to the doctor." She addressed the daughter, "Your mother is a very special woman. May you grow up good and strong like her."

The young woman smiled shyly. She propped her mother up as best she could.

"Will you be alright, *Mama?*" Ida asked.

The woman nodded and she and her daughter began their ascent up the steep mountainside.

Ida stared after them. "Thank you," she shouted.

Glad for the impetus of gravity, the journey back was quicker than the trip up. She stopped as she came to the riverside and inspected the area up and down the river. No youth. She dropped her aching body onto the beach and sat there with her eyes closed.

Oh, to open her eyes and find herself back home. She raised her head and looked into the silent faces of the children circling her. Promise reached out and stroked her hair.

"*Mama*, get up. We can go now."

Ida closed her hand around the little fingers and drew them to her lips. Like replacing dirty dish water with clean, the ache receded and love flooded in. She stole a moment to savor it. Then a pair of hands reached out to help her up.

"Samson." She took in the boy she thought she'd left behind. "You are a clever boy."

He grinned. "You need a man to look after you."

She took his hands and stood up. "Thank you. You saved the woman's life." She stared into the big eyes. "I am so proud of you."

Moses shook her arm, pointing to Surprise. He lay under the weeping willow tree, coughing.

"We need to keep going," she said. She swung the child onto her back and tied him on with the tablecloth.

CHAPTER 12

"Estelle!" Japie screamed his daughter's name as he stumbled across the manicured lawn, leapt over the border of azaleas, toward the pool. His thoughts flew to the picture on the front of today's Star: A child who drowned in the family pool yesterday. He was only two.

Please God, don't let her be in the pool. A few more strides along the bricked path to the pool, through the open gate. He slid to a stop. The pool was empty. Within the fenced in area–no one. The pool net lay abandoned on the grass. He swept around, scanning the rest of the garden facing the gate.

"Estelle. *Waar is jy?* Where are you?"

Just then Edward appeared from behind the rockery in the far corner of the garden. In his hand a garden rake, the top broken and dangling at an angle. Clumps of grass and moist, dark earth jammed between its long iron teeth. The gardener looked up guiltily at the broken rake.

Japie heart froze. "What did you do to Estelle?" He rushed around the rock garden when he saw a pair of size four running shoes sticking out. He sprinted to her side where she lay spread out on the lawn. He shook her. "Open your eyes. Estelle, open your eyes."

"Edward. What did you do?" He jumped up suddenly and grabbed the terrified man.

"I am very sorry, *Baas*, I didn't…"

Japie hit him. The man doubled up. Japie's shoe caught the man's chin as he fell forward. Edward flew backward, landing with a thud on the ground. Japie stood over the writhing man.

Edward raised an arm to shield himself. "*Slang.* Snake," he whispered, pointing to the hedge behind him. Japie saw it. The broken, bloodied body of a black mamba. Japie scooped his arms under his little girl and ran toward the house.

"Rene, *kom! Vinnig!* Come quickly!" He yelled. His head buzzed with the horrible sensation of being out of control.

Rene came flying out the front door.

"Call Dr. Grobbelaar at the clinic. Tell him I'm bringing Estelle. She's been bitten by a black mamba."

Rene hesitated.

"*Gou! Gou!*" Japie ran through the French doors, scooped up the car keys as he rushed past the telephone table, the child bouncing in his arms. Rene raced behind him, dialing the number on her cell phone as she ran. Japie placed the child in her arms in the front seat and they sped off.

At the lights, Japie turned onto the Nelspruit road, grateful for the double lane which would make it easier to pass any slow vehicles. He sped up just as a large furniture removal van eased into his lane to pass a laden, logging truck. Japie slammed his hand on the horn and kept it there. But the driver kept right on driving squarely in front of Japie, keeping a steady pace ahead of him. Oncoming traffic was heavy and Japie couldn't find a gap to pass. He also anticipated the trucks ahead of him would slow down as the incline in the road grew sharply and became a steep hill. Sure enough, both trucks geared down and struggled to gain momentum up the hill.

"Get out the way, you stupid idiot." He hammered the horn and yelled obscenities through the open window of his car. He looked down at his little girl, lying so still and white in her mother's arms. Head bowed and eyes scrunched closed, Rene lips move rapidly. He knew she was praying.

Thank Heaven. There was a gap. He swung the steering-wheel to the right, floored the accelerator and swung sharply into the lane of oncoming traffic then rocked back into his lane, hearing now the angry honking of the driver who missed him. Behind him the furniture van blasted the air. He heard nothing; felt nothing. All that mattered was in the car with him.

Then he heard it: a police siren. No. Not now. The police car came up behind him, lights flashing, siren wailing. He tried to signal to the police he had a sick child in the car. But the other car began to edge him off the road. He swung off the road, hit the gear stick into neutral and jumped out the car. He flew over to the policeman still sitting behind the wheel.

"Please let me go. My little girl's been bitten by a snake."

The man rolled down his window, "I beg your pardon?"

Japie repeated himself. Without missing a beat, the officer clipped in his seatbelt and shouted for his colleague to get in the car. To Japie he said, "Follow me." He checked in his rear view mirror, slid out into the traffic, his siren still running, and led Japie through the traffic.

As Japie screeched into the parking lot of the clinic, two orderlies came running out to meet him with a gurney. They rushed to the car while a white-haired man hurried through the door, deep creases between his eyes.

"You sure it was a black mamba, Japie?"

71

"*Ja*, Dr. Grobbelaar, I saw it." Before they had finished speaking, Estelle had been whisked off, the doctor shuffling after her as fast as his aging legs allowed.

"It's better if you wait in the waiting room, Japie," Dr. Grobbelaar shouted behind him. Japie's body felt like a sopping towel hanging on a peg while haphazard thoughts raced around his brain.

Rene pressed her hands to the side of her face. She stared up at him through her tears. He didn't notice. She put her arms around him. He didn't feel her.

"What happened, Japie?" Rene stared into his eyes. He fixed his eyes on the pale green paint of the waiting room. He said nothing.

"Japie?"

He glanced at her briefly then back to the wall. "She was lying behind the rockery. I thought Edward had killed her."

Rene's head snapped up to look at him, grabbing him by the shoulders. "What did you do, Japie?"

He shoved her hands away. "He'll be alright," Japie said. "For goodness sake, Rene, Estelle's in there dying and you're worried about the gardener."

Rene shook her head. "What happened to the snake?"

"Edward killed it." He turned his back on her.

Rene stepped away. "You beat the man who tried to save your daughter's life?"

That did it. Japie spun round on her. "If you can't support me, get out!"

Rene's eye's filled, her shoulders slumped. She stumbled over to a chair in the corner and fell into it.

Japie's restless footsteps echoed on the tiled floor of the empty waiting room while his wife sat motionless in the corner, her face in her hands. The moments lost definition, slipping into an hour, and still no word from the doctor. Japie needed fresh air. He strode outside into the hot afternoon sun in the parking lot. He pulled out his cigarettes and with trembling fingers lit one. How much longer? He knew a mamba bite on a small child was bad news. They needed a miracle. No news meant that at least she was still alive. Please God… let her live.

Then, Rene came running to the door. "Japie. Come quickly. Dr. Grobbelaar wants to talk to us."

CHAPTER 13

Ida and the children moved on in silence, following the stream as it wound its way down through dense reeds and vegetation. Along this stretch of the path Ida felt the prick of blackjack hooks as the seeds buried themselves into her clothing. Every step rubbed the tiny points against her skin. Time did not allow her to stop to pull them out. Blending into the greenery, too, the Khaki plant filled the air with its pungent odor. Ida felt assaulted from without and within.

She waited while some of the children passed her. As Samson drew abreast of her, she fell in step with him. "What made you come back?"

He kicked aside a loose stone on the path. "I think about my uncle. Why he take everything?" He flung his arms in a wide arc. "Why he not come to get us? I think about Phineas. If I stay, he is alone. Maybe you are right. I must come with you."

Ida stopped in her tracks and faced him, turning his face to look at her. "I am very happy you came with us." He nodded. Together they moved on.

The terrain began to flatten as the stream broadened into a wetland of soggy ground and reeds. The path petered out and Ida veered away from the stream to search for a path away from the marsh. Bandile saw it first.

"It is over there around these rocks," he shouted. The children ran to it, seeing who could get there first. For quite a distance it could be seen winding parallel to the stream.

"Let's keep together," Ida called after them.

A sudden cool breeze whipped around her, catching her by surprise. She looked up. Black clouds had drifted over the sun and the strengthening wind whipped the reeds and grasses before it in a submissive bend. Within minutes she felt the first sting of rain pellets. They needed cover. She searched around for higher land. Ahead lay a *kopje* which looked as though a huge boulder had tumbled from the sky, shattered and scattered over the area. "Run to those rocks over there." She pointed with her chin.

The children ran ahead while she shambled along with Surprise bouncing heavily on her back. "Keep away from that big tree. We don't want to be near it if there's lightning."

Rain exploded like missiles in the sand around her.

73

"*Mama*. Over here." Samson hurried through some bushes, up and over a pile of rocks to a deep depression in the largest rock which looked as though a giant spoon had scooped it out, gouging a wide band some fifteen meters long. Above it a prominent shelf of rock protruded some two meters.

Ida couldn't have ordered better protection from the rain. The last to reach the cave, she pulled Surprise off her back and placed him next to the others. As she scrambled up, the sky violently unplugged, peppering the earth with miniature water bombs. The children huddled close to the front of the cave's broad mouth.

"Go further in," she said, shooing them away from the slashing rain. None of them moved. She noticed them snatch glances at the shadows behind them.

"There is nothing in there," she laughed. The children stayed glued where they were until a gust of wind lifted the curtain of rain and blew it over the children. As one they scrambled backward and pulled their legs away.

A crack of thunder drew all eyes to the small black face of a vervet monkey peeping around a tree trunk growing at the far end of the cave. It shook its head flicking off shiny raindrops that dangled off the end of its fur.

"Don't move," Ida whispered while she studied the monkey out the corner of her eye. "Maybe the monkey will share our shelter with us."

Another giant flash lit up the cave in a blaze of light immediately followed by an almighty crack and a dozen furry black faces suddenly appeared and scampered along a thick root growing along the roof of the rock then disappeared into the deepest part of the cave where they whimpered and chattered in its dank darkness. Animal and human were united in common fear of the storm.

In the stillness that followed, a lone vervet scurried down the smooth bark of the tree trunk. Come on in, little lady.

"Look," Ida whispered. Tiny black hands of a baby gripped the mother's sopping fur, its face hidden in its mother's warmth. The mother vervet bobbed her head in search of the rest of her troop hiding in the darkness. Her eyes checking every now and then on Ida and the children. After several apprehensive attempts to grab the root, she finally stretched out an arm to grab the root and haul herself up when Surprise coughed. In a flash, she disappeared back up the tree. But the next roll of thunder crashing behind her sent the monkey springing down the tree once more, along the root and into the cave to join the others.

Trickles of water began to wear fine tracks down the rock face and pool at the feet of the children. They pressed closer together and further into the cave. Ida lent back against the rock wall allowing her mind to wander back to the incident at the stream.

Out of the chaos of her memories she remembered the youth's shoes–soleless and scuffed, held together only by stubborn stitching. Her mind wandered around the issue, searching for clues to his anger. Of course the alcohol deepened it, but what lay behind it all? Last week she would have said with indignation, "Why aren't these boys looking for a job?" In a few short days here in the community, she knew there had to be a deeper reason, a better question to ask.

What kind of life did he lead? The boy looked into the future, knowing nothing much was going to change his life. Those old shoes would disintegrate as certainly as the hope of a good job. And the anger? Someone had to pay for it. The innocent? The powerless? They were dry flint in the path of anger's firestorm. She sighed. His future was as hopeless as hers was bleak.

She felt someone tug at her arm. Promise.

"The rain, it is almost finished." She sat down next to Ida and leaned against her.

Ida slipped her arm around the child. She looked around her. This was a good time to ration the water and give out the last of the fruit. She reached over to the grocery cart Moses had been so willing to pull behind her. Each child received a small yellow and red mango but her hand came up empty when she searched for one for herself. She tried to ignore the ache in her stomach, aware that hunger was the children's most faithful companion.

She studied the faces of the children and listened to the satisfied smack of lips and slurping tongues as mango juice oozed down dusty smiling faces. Now this felt good. It was a treat for hungry little people and a welcome pleasure for a lonely big person.

As Bandile bit off a small piece of overripe mango peel he threw it in the direction of the monkeys. It started a scuffle. Scores of furry fingers snatched at the peel and fought to take possession of it.

Maybe this wasn't such a good idea after all. Although they stayed in the shadows, Ida could hear the monkeys chattering and shuffling behind them.

"Put the pips and peels in the plastic bag, everyone. We will give them to the monkeys when we leave." In seconds, stringy mango pips plopped into the bag. But the monkeys lost out on the peels. The children had eaten them all.

Then the storm stopped. In the stillness, droplets of water from the rock shelf plopped into puddles of mud while beads of water slid off the leaves of trees and bushes and left the world scrubbed and clean. Dust and grit had melted away, purifying the air.

The children twisted round where they were sitting to view the monkeys but the animals still hid in the darkness.

"Phineas, why don't you throw the pips to the monkeys?" Phineas shrank away, shaking his head. No one wanted the job, so once the children had vacated the cave, Ida lay the bag down and opened it to make it easier for the animals to get at the fruit. She walked away to give them some distance. The monkey mob materialized in the sunshine and in seconds the mango pips were gone. A lone young vervet sat with his hand inside the packet searching. Every now and then, his head would disappear into the packet looking in vain for one last pip.

Aware of the danger of plastic bags to wild animals, Ida went to retrieve the empty bag. But the monkey hadn't given up hope that a snack lay inside there somewhere. He seized it with one hand, gave her an impertinent stare and disappeared into the trees. When he was safe in the topmost branches he peered down at her.

He wasn't coming down and she wasn't going up and they needed to keep moving. Ida rallied the group and they set off along the path now sticky with mud. The stream narrowed through a small gulley of rock, into a sharp dog-leg to the west. Along the riverbank the group picked its way over large boulders littering the path, eyes fixed on where their feet trod. In front, the children slowed down and finally stopped.

Little Agnus reached up her arms to her sister Promise to be lifted up. Promise walked in front of her and bent over, hoisting the child onto her back. Her arms gripped the skinny brown legs, now splattered with thick red mud, and the line moved on.

At last the soil gave way to sand. Glad that this made it easier for Promise to carry Agnus, Ida still wondered how long the older child could carry her sister. As an adult, she herself was taking strain with her load. The constant leaning forward put strain on her neck and her back ached. She slowed down. A tap on her arm from behind her caused her to turn around. Moses pointed to Surprise.

Ida stopped. "I don't understand."

Moses reached out her hands to take Surprise.

"Thank you, Moses, but I can carry him."

Moses pointed to the grocery cart. Ah. Clever kid. Why hadn't she thought of it? Perhaps the cart would be useful after all, now that the food was gone. Lowering Surprise onto the ground, she lined the cart with the tablecloth then twisted the two upper corners around the handle and tucked them inside the cart to increase the area for Surprise to lean on. His weight would keep the cloth in place. She eased him inside. Before his head rested against the cloth his eyes had closed.

Grateful to have her burden off her back, Ida pulled the cart but soon realized she had to bend awkwardly to keep the cart upright. Plus the wet sand sucked at the wheels, increasing the drag on the cart. Finally she gave in to Moses' request to relieve her. Somehow the girl managed better than she did. Ida let her go on ahead.

The sun came out. It was not so fierce now. Ida looked at her watch. Five o'clock. Another hour and a half of sunlight. Maybe they could make it before dark.

The momentum of the stream picked up as the terrain descended down a gradual slope. Ida noticed the neat rows of water-guzzling gum trees on either side of the water. It was good to see this logging company was complying with the regulations to keep the gum trees from growing too close to bodies of water. What a pity so many of these stately trees had had to be chopped down.

The stream now flowed over smooth, flat rocks. Ahead she could see what looked like the start of rapids. The tumble of rushing water grew louder as it sped over smooth beds of rocks. Alongside it, the path meandered through the rocks, becoming more difficult to walk on. The brush became denser and massive trees lined the stream's edge. Following the rumbling stream round a bend to the west, Ida stopped and stared at the scene before her.

The stream emptied into the mouth of a small dam set at the base of a lush valley. Tall, thin gum trees, stripped of their lower branches, grew in neat rows for as far as she could see. From where she was the trees stretched over the entire area surrounding the dam and spread over the hills, an emerald canopy of gigantic moss.

They followed the path around the edge of the dam through knee-high grass until they reached a natural clearing near the water's edge. Ida surveyed the dam. "Let's have a rest under that tree." She pointed to a tree that was easily ten meters tall. Its densely leafed branches spread beneath it a carpet of deep shade. As she approached it she noticed the large thorns growing up its bulbous trunk. A Brazilian kapok. Not so good to lean against but it gave her hope. The tree wasn't indigenous so there must be a homestead or dwellings not too far away.

At her voice, Surprise opened his eyes and stared around him

"Hello, sleepy head," she said in English. "Are you feeling better?" He tried to push himself out of the cart. Ida pulled him out and settled him on a patch of short grass. He felt hot. "Have some water." She raised the bottle to his lips. After a few sips, Ida pulled it away from him. There wasn't much left.

She stretched her aching back. To the west the sun was reaching the tree line. Five minutes; that's all they could afford. They were getting out of there before dark if she had to carry each child on her hands and knees.

Scattered under the shade of the kapok, the children lay resting. "Have some water, then we must move on." Ida called to the children. She measured out a few mouthfuls for each of the children, making sure there was a little left for Surprise. The children went silently back to their positions under the tree. Phineas and Agnus fell instantly asleep. From his pocket, Samson pulled out the page of newspaper he'd been reading earlier. In seconds he was lost in his quest to read.

Promise came over to Ida and talked quietly. "The little ones, they are tired."

"We need to get to my house before the sun sets, Promise." She peered into the worried face of the girl. "The quicker we get home, the sooner we can eat and drink and rest." She checked her watch, holding out five fingers. "Five minutes."

Promise wandered off to Agnus and plopped down beside her. She lifted the sleeping child's head onto her lap and closed her eyes.

Ida found a space in the shade and lay back. She, too, closed her eyes and felt some of the anxiety drain from her. For a few minutes the soft lap of water and the occasional 'coorr coorr' of a dove's call were the only sounds.

An explosive snort and whoosh of water broke the silence. Ida shot up. Two bulbous red rimmed eyes stared at her from the surface of the water only meters away. Then a cavernous pink mouth erupted above the surface of the dam flaunting two pairs of foot-long tusks. The hippo tossed his head from side to side, bellowing his call of territorial dominance and his need for instantaneous compliance. The children submitted to his display with a united scream and fled.

Ida crept backward, not knowing if she should look the animal in the eyes or lower them to lessen her threat to it; but she wasn't staying to find out. After all she'd been through, she wasn't ending up a hippo-kill statistic. She turned and sped after the children.

A snatched look behind her—ripples ringed the area where the hippo had been. That could be good. But then it could be bad. What if he lived up to his reputation of being a nasty, stubborn son of the river? Where was he? Following the sounds of the children ahead of her she sped through the grass. Another glance back to the water. No hippo. Thank you. Thank you. She caught herself. Who was she thanking? She stopped, holding her sides.

Between gasps she shouted to the children, "He's gone."

They began to trickle back to her. She counted them. Six, seven, eight. Someone was missing.

"Surprise." She charged back the way they'd come. "Surprise, where are you?" Behind her she heard the children calling.

Moses caught up to Ida and flashed past. She flew from bush to rock to clump of tall grass, her neck thrust forward. Searching. She would stop to listen then charge on again.

Ida felt a tug on her arm. It was Samson. "The hippo," he said, "maybe he find Surprise?"

Ida stared at him. Impossible. But was it? She shook her head. "Come on, Samson. Help me find him."

"He is here!"

Ida swung round to face the direction of Moses' voice. The

79

anthill. Rounding the mound of bush-covered earth, Ida cried out when she saw him. Moses kneeled next to the inert body of Surprise, stroking the tiny black curls now sprinkled with pale grains of sand. Baggy pants dwarfed his scrawny chicken legs stretched out in front of him. Ida flung herself beside Moses and reached for his pulse. She couldn't feel any.

The rest of the children arrived and jostled Ida to get a closer look.

"Move back. I need space." Ida probed around Surprise's neck for his pulse. She slumped forward. "Thank God. I found it."

Flashing a look at Moses, Ida was struck by the lack of emotion on the girl's face. She appeared neither happy nor sad... until a tear leaked out the corner of her eye. Ida grabbed Moses' hand. "He's going to be okay."

She turned back to Surprise. "He's hot." she said. "Who's got the water bottle?" No one had it. "See if you can find the water-bottle, Moses."

Moses sat very still. Her eyes scanned the surface of the water. She seemed satisfied the hippo was no longer a danger and raced off in the direction of the kapok tree. Within seconds she returned with the bottle. While Ida hoisted up Surprise's head, Moses pried the bottle between his lips. His eyes opened.

"We thought you went to swim with the hippo." Ida feathered the sand off his face and smiled. He reached up for the bottle with both hands and gulped the water down with surprising strength. Ida pried the bottle away from him. "We must leave some for later." But the water was finished. They had to find more. The old expression came to Ida: "Water, water, everywhere, and not a drop to drink."

Ida drew the children together. "I know you are tired but Surprise is very sick. We must keep going." She looked at her watch. "Moses. Bandile. How much further to my house?" Moses stared along the direction of the stream. She indicated the range of hills at the far side of the dam, using her hands to show the house was just beyond them.

"We have to go through those hills?" Ida said. Moses nodded.

CHAPTER 14

Ida and the children approached the gap between the hills through which the stream ran. Before them, an explosion of rich green vegetation spread as far as they could see. Immense trees lined the banks of the stream. Like bodybuilders holding out their weights, their branches reached over the rushing water to link up with others from the other side.

How were they to negotiate this lot? Stunning to look at, but where was the track through it? It was snake heaven. A tangled maze of tall, thick grasses grew between boulders and thickets, lying randomly between the trees. Ida asked the children to wait while she went to investigate a way through to the other side of the valley.

"*Mama?*" Bandile called after her.

"In a minute." She headed off in a new direction. A dead end.

"*Mama?*" Bandile asked.

"What is it?" Her voice came from behind a grove of Bushwillow.

He ran up to her and slipped his hand into hers. "I can show you."

She threw back her head. "Of course. You were here," she said. "You just earned ice-cream tonight." Hopefully there was still some left.

Bandile pulled her toward a towering yellow fever tree. "We went this way." She'd missed it. Between the tree and the stream, a patch of marsh reeds masked the beginning of a path, part of which she could now see winding through the valley.

"Over here," she called to the children.

She surveyed the path. Hauling Surprise in the cart over this rugged terrain was not an option. She tied him to her back and set off, followed by the rest of the children with Moses carrying the cart.

"Don't be so careful watching out for snakes that you slip on these rocks," Ida said. She fanned the long grass and reeds before her like a blind person with a cane searching for anything that slithered, crawled or ran on four legs.

After fifteen minutes of slogging along the track, and not a moment too soon for Ida, the rocks gradually gave way to flatter ground, which then burst through the wall of trees to an undulating plain of young pine trees. Ida gasped. In the middle distance to the west of the stream she recognized the granite koppie she looked out onto whenever she sat on her veranda enjoying a hot cup of tea. Not more than twenty minutes, if they hurried, and they'd be home.

As she turned around to tell the children, she became aware that Surprise's weight had shifted to the left, threatening to drag her sideways. She bent the opposite way to help him readjust his position but he didn't move.

"Surprise, do you sleep?" She patted his rump and jiggled him. He remained a dead weight on her back.

Moses moved closer to inspect the situation. She slapped him firmly on the back. He didn't move.

"Help me get him off." Ida undid the table cloth and with Moses' help lowered the child onto the ground. Please let him be okay. We're so close.

Surprise lay with his eyes closed, his mouth open and his lips dry and cracked. Where was she going to get clean water? The child needed it now. She collapsed beside him feeling as though the last bit of strength was leaving her. Her head fell into her hands. The soft breeze of evening fanned her tired, aching body. For a few moments she tried to run away into the secret places of her soul–to hide from the war raging in her mind. But the butterfly touch of Promise's hand on her shoulder drew her back to the present. She was afraid the little girl would see in her eyes the defeat she felt. She dropped her gaze and ran her fingers through her curls thinking, "God help me. I'm so tired."

Surprise groaned beside her, rescuing her from her thoughts. Pushing herself up, she surveyed the area. Ahead of them there was no sign of life. Surely they weren't too far from the first group of houses in her home area of Riverside?

"*Mama*," Promise tugged at her skirt. "Look. Look."

Ida turned to the east and slightly behind them. A thin spiral of blue smoke not fifty meters away curled lazily into the air. She couldn't have been paying attention. The splinter of hope that entered her mind brought a shot of adrenalin. Where there's smoke there are people.

"Moses, please dip the table cloth in the stream. When it is very wet, wipe Surprise's body all over with it. We must cool him down." Her movements indicated what to do. Turning to Samson, she said, "Come with me. We're going to find clean water."

Like swimming the breaststroke, they parted the long grass before them, listening to the swish and slap as it whipped against their body and legs. Ida kept her eyes focused on the smoke. Samson followed a step behind her. The grass suddenly ended a few meters later bringing them onto a well-worn path leading right to the door of a small brick house. On an ancient kitchen chair sat an equally ancient old man. His rheumy eyes opened wide when he saw them. He pushed himself up upright, his right hand clutching a wooden cane and he swayed onto his feet.

"*Sawubona, Mkhulu,* grandfather," Ida called. "*Kunjani?*"

"*Ng'kona, Mama.*" The corner of the old man's mouth stretched tiredly across the parchment of his face.

"*Mkhulu,* I need some clean water. I have a sick child back there." She pointed behind her.

The old man nodded and tottered to the door, dragging a stiff leg behind him. He hauled himself up onto a step of loose bricks and then through the door. His voice floated out to them. A muted stream of words came from inside the house. He must be lonely. He reappeared a few seconds later with a chipped tin mug which he handed to Ida. He stuck out a stubbled chin, sprinkled with white, in the direction of a water tap next to rows of cabbage and kale growing in trim rows near the house. "The water it is good. It is from the farmer's well."

"*Ngiyabonga.* I thank you, *Mkhulu.* I will send one of the children to bring your mug back."

The old man held up crooked fingers in acknowledgement then lowered himself onto his chair. His eyes lost their interest and he stared, unseeing, ahead.

The water gushed out clear and cold into the mug. Ida handed it to Samson. Then bending over the tap she captured it in her upturned palm and slurped it deeply and long. It poured down the sides of her mouth, down her arms, cascading onto her blouse. She drank until her stomach ached.

Samson reached out for more.

Ida remembered Surprise. "We must go now." She filled the bottle and mug and turned to head back when a loud moan came from inside the old man's house. The old man stumbled inside. She heard him speak. Another deep moan.

Ida looked back in the direction of the children and back again.

"Run carefully," she said to Samson, "Give the mug to Surprise. Do not let him drink too fast. Share the bottle with the rest of the children. If there is not enough we can get some more."

She watched him go, then dashed over to doorway to the house. At first she could see nothing inside the room until her eyes adjusted to the dim light. Then, against the far wall, she saw the skeletal body of a man shivering on a pile of rags. She took a deep breath and held it to keep the putrid odor from entering her lungs.

"*Mkhulu*," she scrunched her eyes against the almost physical onslaught of the foul reek. "Who is this?"

The person on the floor made a faint movement of the head as if trying to look at her. The whites of his enormous brown eyes were dull and dirty brown as a mesh of burst blood vessels covered them. They stared out of a face whose flesh had long since shrunk and toughened to a leathered shroud stretched tight over cavernous cheekbones and strong jaw.

"He is my first born." The old man leaned on his stick at the side of his sick son, his stiff leg stretched out so he could bend down. The old man fumbled with a dirty rag swiping at the yellow vomit that dribbled out the younger man's mouth.

"Why is he not in hospital?" Ida spoke from behind her hand, her eyes wide.

"We have no money." Pressing his hand against his knee he pushed himself to a standing position but would not meet Ida's gaze. "I work with the chickens, and my son, but now I am too old and he is sick."

Just then Samson came running to the house. "*Mama*. Come quickly. Surprise he is not drinking."

Ida took a step backward but addressed the old man. "*Mkhulu*," she glanced back at Samson. "I will see if I can get some help for your son. I still have a long way to get home and the child is sick but I will not forget you."

The old man raised his eyes and looked right into Ida's. "God will bless you."

"What is the name of this farm?"

"*Goedgenoeg Plaas.*" 'Good Enough Farm.' No, it wasn't good enough. Not for these two men. Ida waved to *Mkhulu* and took off. Something nagged at her. She knew that name from somewhere.

Can't think of it now. She let it go.

When she reached the children Moses sat on the red soil holding Surprise's head in her lap, trying to coax water into his mouth. The boy moved his head from side to side in an attempt to get away from the mug.

"Has he drunk any of it?" Ida said.

Moses indicated half a cup. It was better than nothing.

"Samson, please return the mug to *Mkhulu* with our thanks," Ida said. "We will start walking. It is not far to go now." As she scooped Surprise up and swung him onto her back she wondered if her home was as close as she thought. She was learning that distance in the bush was deceptive. "Let's go," she said. The children fell in line and the party set off again.

Hearing odd murmurs of conversation behind her gave Ida a sense of connection with the children, almost like they were family. She felt a wave of warmth flow over her.

Directly ahead, an enormous tree trunk had recently fallen over and blocked the path. It must have been the big storm the other night—the leaves on the tree were still green. She turned around to wait for the children to catch up so she could help them over it.

Bringing up the rear, some distance from the rest of the children, Samson and Moses stood and faced each other, engrossed in an animated conversation. Even from this distance Ida could see something was wrong. Samson hugged his body, his arms jerked out periodically to make a point. What was he saying?

Ida slipped through the children, careful not to draw their attention to what she was doing. She made her way toward Moses and Samson. The chatter behind her became subdued. Samson, too, seemed to become aware of the silence. His face turned toward her. He'd seen her approach. A quick whisper and he grabbed Moses' hand and pulled her along the path toward Ida.

Ida held up her palm, indicating for them to stop. As they reached her, she sank down onto the path and patted the ground next to her. "Sit," she ordered. She glanced over at the other children. They'd lost interest. Bandile kneeled on top of the downed tree trunk, his arms stretched down to pull the younger ones up. They, in turn, jostled each other and yelled to be first.

In front of Ida, Samson faced the bush while Moses doodled in the sand. Ida wondered how to say this. "Samson, have I been a good friend to you?"

He nodded.

"Have I hurt you?"

A vigorous shake of the head.

"*Uyakholwa kimi, na*? Do you believe in me?"

"*Yebo.*"

"If I am your friend, please tell me what is wrong."

He pulled his outstretched legs up to his chest and rested his chin on his knees.

"Samson?" Ida said quietly.

Moses nudged him with her toe.

The boy stared back at her. She nodded.

"You must not send us back to our house."

"Why?" Ida waited.

"In two days it is full moon."

"I cannot hear you well," Ida rolled onto her knees and gently pulled his face toward her.

"It is time for the men to come."

"Which men?"

"They make the girls cry." He shook his head.

Ida's stomach began to churn. "Who are the men?"

"There is one man. He bring his friends. He come when the moon is full."

"Why does he come at full moon?

"We have no lights."

Ida steeled herself against reacting. "Do you know the names of the men?"

A shake of the head.

"Can you tell me anything about him or his friends?"

The children stared at each other. Moses prodded Samson.

"The man speaks with soft voice but his heart is a rock."

"What does he look like?"

"He is big man." That narrowed it down to a few thousand.

"Does he wear glasses? How does he dress?"

Moses became agitated. She stood up and pointed ahead of them. Ida knew she was trying to tell her something but her pantomime wasn't working.

"I'm sorry, Moses. I don't know what you're trying to say."

The girl tried again.

Ida attempted a guess. "Someone is driving a car?"

Moses' eyes lit up and she nodded.

"The man comes to you in a car?"

Moses nodded rapidly and looked at her with expectation. When Ida said nothing more, the girl's head sank onto her chest and the hope in her face seeped out. She shook her head.

"I'm sorry Moses." Ida stood up and grabbed hold of Moses' hand to pull her up. There'd be time to talk about this later. "Some other time. I promise you, Samson and Moses, I will not send you back to your house. I will help you."

"*Mama?*" Samson tugged at her arm. "The man he is important."

I'm sure he thinks he is, Ida thought, but said, "Thank you for telling me. It's getting late and we must go."

As the sun tipped the horizon, they rounded a bend in the stream and there it was. The wild fig tree bowed over by the storm, its branches now pulled through the water by its steady flow. Ida glanced over to the blue container still trembling on churning water. It struck her. It was just two days ago yet a lifetime of experiences away. The moment she had reached down and hauled Moses out of the box she had unwittingly changed the course of her life. How could she explain the paradox of the most wonderful, frightening, energizing, helplessly-hopeful time of her life? She'd taken a detour in her life and found her way back only to find the single thing about her that remained the same was her name.

In a burst of energy Ida ran to her garden gate. She scrabbled in her bag for her bunch of keys. Into the padlock she thrust the key. "We made it." She swung open the gate and flung her arms wide to welcome the children but only Bandile and Moses stood next to her. The rest of the children huddled together under the wild fig tree, looking as though they were going to bolt at the first sign of trouble.

CHAPTER 15

Rene van Reenen stroked the tubby fingers and mouthed a prayer. She stared into the face of her little girl, so tiny and still in the big hospital bed. Her tank of tears had run out during the night and been replaced by a boiler of rage. Right now, she knew that two people were fighting for dominance inside her. The loving mother, and the angry wife. If she didn't get a grip on things, the one would overtake the other, and Estelle would be caught in the middle of deep ugliness.

She wanted to cry, "Enough. I can't take anymore." But where could she go? How could she take Estelle away from the Daddy who loved her?

Japie returned with two steaming cups of tea. He handed one to Rene. Without a word, she took the cup and put it on the small table next to the bed. The tips of her fingers went back to tracing the outline of Estelle's hand.

"Have your tea before it gets cold," Japie said, a sliver of sheepishness appearing on his face.

She said nothing.

For a while they sat in silence, listening to the clattering and muted chattering of a hospital waking up.

"Why don't you go home and have a bath," Japie said. He bent down to look up in her face. "You'll feel better."

She remained motionless.

He stiffened. "You're so ungrateful. I bring you a cup of tea. I suggest you go for a bath and you don't have the decency to speak to me."

"Whatever."

"Look, Rene," his cheeks became red. "How many times have I told...? Where are you going?"

Rene rose silently and slipped behind the curtain.

"Come back here. I'm talking to you." He chased after her. "There you go again. Running off when I'm trying to talk to you. Rene, come back here and talk to me."

Rene hurried to the end of the hallway and snatched a look behind her. Japie rounded the corner into the hallway behind her, smack into someone hurrying from the opposite direction.

"Dr. Grobbelaar?" she heard Japie say. "*Ek is jammer.* I'm sorry."

"*Hoe gaan dit,* Japie, how are you?" Dr. Grobbelaar said. "I'll be coming to see you in about ten minutes."

Rene followed a passageway that turned right and led her away from reception. The rest of Japie's conversation with the doctor was lost to her.

Just five minutes. She needed to pull herself together before she said something she was going to regret. She escaped through a door into a small courtyard open to the sky. Somewhat protected from view was a bench on which she sat.

For a moment the vibrant orange and purple bird-of-paradise flowers growing in the centre of the garden, surrounded by grasses and tropical plants, attracted her attention. Where was the color in her life? Who even knew or cared?

"Rene?"

She shrank against the back of the bench and sat immobilized until his footsteps faded. Retreating into her inner world she found a measure of peace. When she thought about it, it wasn't peace exactly. It was more like the absence of turmoil. Here she didn't have to think about all the things she did that irritated Japie. She could be kind to herself and forget the criticism, the nagging, the expectations. For a little while.

The footsteps returned. "Rene?" She waited a few seconds for him to pass. Stealing one more moment of quiet, she sighed and then stood up. She followed her husband at a distance.

Returning to the ward, she found Dr. Grobbelaar bending over Estelle. Japie stood on the other side of the bed with his arms folded and a frown creasing his face. His head snapped up as she entered. His expression said, "Where the heck were you?"

"Hello, Dr. Grobbelaar." She conjured up a smile.

"*Mama?*" Estelle lay back against the pillows, the starched sheets surrounding her as unruffled as when she'd first been placed on them. Plump arms rose–outstretched.

Rene ran around the doctor and fell across the bed, enveloping her baby in her arms. "*My skattie.* My darling." As she began to laugh a new batch of tears arrived, drenching them both.

Japie, too, sprang forward and gripped the tiny hand around Rene's neck. His eyes filled but he kept his mouth clenched tight.

"Japie and Rene," Dr. Grobbelaar said. "This is one lucky little girl. We think the snake's fangs only grazed her leg and we got her in time. After what Japie has told me and reading between the lines, I believe your gardener hit the snake just as it was striking. Personally, I think he saved Estelle's life."

Rene twisted her head round to stare at Japie. He looked defiantly at Rene but when her gaze blazed into his, he put his head down.

"We'll need to observe her until we're sure she has no complications. If all goes well, you can take her home later this evening."

"*Dankie*. Thank you," both parents said. With one last look the doctor left.

Rene shoved the toxic relationship once more into the cellar of her mind and closed the door.

"*Dankie. Dankie*," she closed her eyes, facing the ceiling. She had her little girl back.

She'd keep the peace–as she'd always done. But she knew she was merely keeping peace. She didn't have the tools to be a peacemaker.

CHAPTER 16

Ida could hear Surprise thrashing around in her bedroom next to the kitchen. Her hand tightened around the phone she held to her ear. With the other hand she stabbed at a smooth blob of congealed paint on the table which she'd never got round to removing. Please answer the phone. In her bedroom she could hear Surprise's muttering growing more agitated and Moses shushing him gently in his delirium.

At the far end of her small house the murmurs of the children in the lounge reached her. What were they doing? She bent forward to peer through the open door. Phineas, and the three little girls, Zinhle, Agnus and Goodness, lay sprawled on the carpet, motionless in sleep. The three older children crowded together in front of the TV, their noses just inches away from the screen watching the SABC 2 news–in English.

It had taken patient persuasion and explanation before Ida had convinced the children to come inside her house. Arriving at her home had been the easy part. The unknown proved to be unexpectedly difficult for them.

"No one is going to chase you away or hurt you," she said, with nods of agreement from Moses and Bandile. "We will lock the doors and you will eat every day." Promise had been the first to step through the gate. She took Ida's hand and beckoned her younger sisters to come, too.

Samson stared at the house as though trying to see though its walls.

"I need someone to look after me," Ida said. For a few moments Ida waited for him, then watched as the tension in his face dissolved into a smile. They all trooped in.

Grateful that was behind her now, Ida waited for someone to answer her phone call. She pressed the phone against her temple. Everything in her cried out to stop, eat, bathe, and sleep for a hundred years. But Surprise's fever had spiked to 40 °C after their simple meal of tinned soup and buttered bread. She dialed the number again. Someone picked up the phone.

"Shelly?" she said when her friend answered. Thank goodness. "Would it be possible for you to come to my house and watch some children for me while I go out?"

"What children?"

"I don't have time to explain everything now ..."

Shelly was apologetic. "Ida, I'm so sorry. I'm next door at Sharon's. I'm babysitting the two bigger kids. She's taken the little guy to the clinic. He's got croup. Jonathon is away on business."

Ida sighed and put down the phone. Next she tried Tracey. But no one answered. They must have already gone to their evening church service. No point trying Gill. She was away visiting family.

At that moment Moses came into the room. Ida put down the phone. "I can't find anyone to stay with you while I take Surprise to the clinic," she said.

Moses pointed to herself and then to the children.

"You'll look after the children?"

Moses nodded.

Ida drew her close, "You're a star, Moses."

A quick list of instructions for bed time and sleeping arrangements and Moses disappeared into the lounge while Ida picked up the phone again. Now to find a ride to the clinic.

She dialed the Nelsons down the street. Five year old Stephanie answered. Sorry. Her parents were out at a movie tonight. She was watching *The Lion King* with Josie. Did Ida want to come and watch too? Ida graciously declined.

When she thought of the Van Reenens next door, she could feel the sudden tension grab her neck. Pull yourself together. What are they going to do to you? She dialed. No answer. That was strange. They always played cards on Sunday night. Feelings of desperation began to rise to the surface. She was running out of options. There was Mr. Nkosi two doors down. Maybe he would help.

A man's voice answered after the first ring. "Mr. Nkosi? It's Ida Morgan from up the road." She explained her dilemma. At last. Mr. Nkosi said he would be outside her gate in five minutes.

Ida put down the phone and ran to her bedroom. She hurried to the linen cupboard dragged out a light blanket which she threw over Surprise and scooped him up in weary arms. Walking past the lounge she saw that Bandile now lay slumped against the TV table, the next victim of sleep.

"I am taking Surprise to see the doctor," Ida said to Samson and Promise, who hadn't moved an inch since she'd seen last them.

"Moses will look after you until I get back." The children's eyes never left the screen. Ida smiled and moved on.

By the time the gate closed behind her Mr. Nkosi had driven up and jumped out to open the back door for her. He stopped short when he saw the child. He stared at her. "I thought..."

She smiled when she saw his face. "It's a long story."

Mr. Nkosi began to laugh. "You are the first white person I have heard speak my language. I have heard some do but I have never heard it myself." Along the way, Ida filled him in on some of the events of the past two days. He listened without interrupting, stopping her only every now and then to ask for clarification. When they finally arrived at the clinic, Ida was grateful Surprise had fallen into a more natural sleep. Mr. Nkosi ran around the car and took the child from her to the waiting room.

Six other people were waiting to be attended to.

As they walked up to reception desk an orderly came in, staring at the chart in his hand.

"Mary Bongani?"

A young woman rose clutching a bloody cloth to her temple and followed him.

Ida turned to the receptionist. "We have a little boy who is very sick."

"Yes, when you have given me your details the doctor will see him." She went back to her work.

"How long do you think it will be?" Ida said.

"You have five people before you." The receptionist slid over a form to fill in.

"But the child is very sick. He needs to see someone straight away."

"Madam, these people are also sick. They have been waiting a long time."

Ida completed the form and fell into an armchair next to Mr. Nkosi. She reached over to take the sleeping Surprise who lay across his lap.

"Mr. Nkosi," she started.

"My name is Stanley." The corners of his mouth turned up.

"Stanley, I can't thank you enough for helping me tonight."

"It is a pleasure." Slowly he rose with the child and lowered him into Ida's arms.

"I will ask my wife Ponso to stay with the other children tonight. I leave for Barberton at five in the morning, so my wife will take our children with her to your house. If that's okay?"

Ida looked up into the man's kind face. "Of course. Thank you."

Ida stared after him as he left through the front doors. So many good people around. She suddenly became aware of a woman hurrying past her, down the hallway toward the exit, blowing her nose loudly. Her red, swollen eyelids were smudged with black mascara. As the woman stopped momentarily to search in her handbag for a clean tissue, her light brown hair fell in front of her face. But it was the tinkle of gold bracelets as her slim hands scratched around her bag that caused Ida to catch her breath.

"Rene?"

Rene's van Reenen's head snapped up. As she saw Ida, her hand shot up to hide her tears. Before she could say anything, Japie appeared behind her his breathing labored.

"Rene, what are you doing?" He grabbed hold of her arm and tried to pull her back the way she'd come. She became rigid and stood her ground.

Japie caught sight of Ida, stared at her for a second then turned his attention back to his wife. "Stop making a scene," he said between clenched teeth.

"I need some fresh air." Rene's words came out softly but she yanked at the hand gripping her arm.

"Estelle needs you," he said loudly, his grasp on her tightening.

Rene glanced around the waiting room at all the people staring at them. Her eyes lost their fire and became vacant. The starch of tension that had kept her body rigid dissipated, leaving behind an empty collapsing shell. She followed him, a beaten dog following its master.

Ida stared after them. Pressure had a way of exposing the real person. When she thought about it, she wasn't really surprised. The guy was a prize jerk. But what was wrong with little Estelle? It wasn't the ideal time to find out.

Surprise groaned softly. The large, elderly woman in the next chair twisted around, took her hand off her walking stick and gently patted his shoulder with stiff, pudgy fingers.

"Shhh. Shhh," she said. Below the faded cloth wrapped around her tight black curls, Ida noticed the whites of her dark eyes were tinged with brown where sun and dust had rubbed the whiteness out. The old woman whispered to Ida, "Shame."

Ida nodded. Only then did Ida notice the woman's problem. At the end of her blotchy and bloated leg, where her skin was stretched to breaking point, her foot rotated limply so that it rested sideways on the floor. Each time she moved, the woman took in a quick intake of air. The poor woman.

"How long have you been waiting?" Ida said.

"I am here four hours." When she saw Ida's horrified look she continued, "But I am the next one."

Surprise's head began to whip from side to side. His arms flayed out while he moaned. A sheen of moisture covered his face. Ida stared up at the receptionist hoping she noticed what was going on. The woman kept her eyes on her work.

Just then the orderly came in. "Maria Msasa?" He looked around the room.

The old lady next to Ida raised her hand. "I am Maria but this boy is very sick. Let him go first."

Ida felt her throat tighten. She reached out a hand and squeezed the old woman's hand. "Thank you. Thank you." She followed the man.

The orderly pulled aside the pale blue curtain surrounding the cubicle and motioned for Ida to place Surprise on the bed.

"So, what have we here?" A short, bald man in a white coat strode in. His face told a different story to his cheerful voice. He wore weariness like a drooping daffodil. He studied the chart in his hand.

"My name is Dr. Labuschagne." He bent over Surprise and his smile faded. He felt Surprise's pulse then listened to his heart. "What's the matter, little man?" His voice was soft. He checked the chart again. "Mrs. Morgan?"

She turned to him.

"We need to do some tests. Please will you wait in the waiting-room? We'll let you know as soon as we know what's going on."

Ida slipped out and went in search of comfort in a cup of tea. Maybe the small cafeteria was still open. It was. She took her tea back to the waiting room, relieved to notice the old woman was no longer in the waiting-room.

Half an hour later, the doctor appeared. She jumped up.

"Mrs. Morgan, Surprise is a very sick little boy."

"What's wrong with him?"

"He has malaria."

She felt herself relax. "Thank goodness."

He said nothing.

She searched his face.

He did not return her gaze.

The porcupine was backing in. "You think something else is wrong?"

"Let's wait and see. We'll monitor him overnight. We'll let you know as soon as the tests come back." He rested his hand briefly on her shoulder and left.

Ida slumped into the chair. A few days ago her life had been predictable and comfortable. Now a war raged inside her. Interestingly, the war told her she was alive. The pain was no longer for herself. A deep sadness filled her, not for the past, but for the possibility of a future cut short. A little boy had charmed his way into her heart and it hurt.

A soft tap on her shoulder startled her. She closed her drooping mouth and rubbed her eyes. She must have fallen asleep. Had she been snoring?

The nurse waited. "You can see him now." She led Ida down a maze of passages to Ward A and pointed to bed 2. "He's sleeping."

Ida passed the only other bed in the ward, also screened by a drawn curtain. From behind the curtain came the soft wheezing sound of a child with a blocked nose plus the murmur of two people talking.

Arriving at bed 2, Ida pulled aside the drapes and there he was. He lay on his stomach with his thin legs tucked under him so that his rear-end stuck up in the air. His face was turned toward Ida, his mouth open, relaxed in sleep. His left arm stretched out, a nasty IV jammed into his tiny hand.

Ida pulled a chair closer to the bed. She drew the sheet over him then reached under it for his hand. Fighting with all that was left of her will-power, she managed to keep her eyes open for few moments. But when her head fell onto the edge of the bed she fought it no more. She slept.

Five o'clock the next morning the rattle of a medicine trolley woke her. She stretched stiffly.

"Good morning, Mrs. Morgan," a smiling nurse greeted her. "You must have been very tired. You have been lying in the same position all night."

The voice wakened Surprise. He looked around him at the strange nurse and the attachments to his body. His mouth puckered and trembled.

Ida took his hand. "*Sawubona*, Surprise. I am here."

He held on tight and examined his surroundings.

"Moses and Bandile are waiting for you to get better and come home." The tautness in his body softened. "Are you hungry?"

He nodded.

Just then footsteps sounded down the hallway. Dr. Labuschagne's tired face appeared around the curtain. Surprise reached out to Ida, panic in his eyes.

"It is okay," she gave him a hug then pried him gently away from her. "This is the doctor. He wants to make you better."

"Hello, little man," Dr. Labuschagne said, closing the curtain behind him. "How are you feeling this morning?"

Ida translated for Surprise. He pressed his head against the pillow and stared at the drip-stand next to his bed.

"He seems much better," Ida said.

There was a pause as the doctor fiddled with the chart. Finally, he said, "Mrs. Morgan, we have his tests back."

She saw his face and felt a tightening in her chest.

"I'm afraid he has AIDS."

CHAPTER 17

Ida felt like she'd been dumped onto the beach by a giant wave at spring tide. No sooner had one wave battered her into the sand when another followed close behind, threatening to drown her in the roiling waters of her emotions. She needed air. If only there was someone she could talk to.

She sat in the corner of the clinic's cafeteria, digging patterns into the Styrofoam cup of tea with her nails, while she waited for Surprise to be released. What was she going to do about him? Was she capable of taking care of a sick child?

What of all the other children? She couldn't help them all. Her thoughts moved on. Thank goodness for Mrs. Nkosi. Ponso. What would she have done without her help?

She suddenly remembered. She needed to phone Sergeant Jawena, but first she had to find a ride home. She pulled out her cell. It said, "You have three seconds airtime left."

She hurried over to the woman behind the counter. "I don't suppose you sell airtime?"

The woman shook her head. Drat.

"Please would you give me change for R20?" She handed over her last note. "Is there a public phone I can use?" The woman dumped the change into her hand and pointed to a booth at the entrance to the restroom. She thanked the woman and moved off.

Shelly Link's number was as familiar to her as her own front teeth. Everyone needed a friend like Shelly. When Shelly answered, Ida briefly explained the events of the last few days and her present dilemma. She waited. Silence. "Shelly, are you there?" More silence. "Shelly?"

"Ida, you're joking?"

"No, I need to go back to Masoyi and get my car."

"I don't know what to say. How did you…?"

"Shelly, I have another call to make and I'm running out of money. I'll tell you all about it when I see you. I know it's short notice but can you help me?"

Another pause. "*Ja*. I'll be there in about an hour. Okay?"

"You're the best. Thank you." Ida replaced the receiver and searched in her diary for Sergeant Jawena's phone number.

Once she'd dialed the number she waited for someone to call the

Sergeant to the phone. The moments ticked by. She pushed in another R2. She was about to put in another two, when, "Sergeant Jawena here."

Thank goodness. "This is Ida Morgan."

He remembered her.

"Sergeant, some things have happened since you came to my house. Remember the child who ran away? Well, more children are at my house now and they need help." Briefly she told him about the children and what they'd finally told her about the men.

There was silence on the other side of the phone. She dropped in another R2. "Sergeant?"

"Mrs. Morgan, this is not good. I need time to work out the best way to deal with it. You are sure the children have their facts correct? If we are to help them, we must be sure."

"They are adamant the men come every full moon and Friday is full moon. It's our best opportunity to catch the men. Once they know the children are gone they won't be back; then we'll never find them." Another thought hit her. "Until they hurt other children."

"It is true, Mrs. Morgan. These men are open graves for children to fall into. We will get them."

"One more thing, Sergeant. Something has definitely happened to Simeon Phiri, the young man I was telling you about. He still hasn't returned and I'm worried about him. Would you look into it for me?" The phone began to beep. "Sergeant, I must go. I have no more change to put in the phone."

"I am in my car. What is the phone number there?"

"I can't read it. Someone's written graffiti over it but I should be home from the hospital by lunch…" The phone cut off. Well, at least she'd said what she needed to.

Ida replaced the phone, immensely relieved the police were taking the kids seriously and would deal with it. She returned to her table to find her tea had been whipped away. She headed to the counter for another cup when she remembered she had no more change.

She sat down and looked longingly at the tea counter. The woman behind the counter appeared at her side, holding another Styrofoam cup. "I'm sorry, I thought you had gone. Here is a fresh cup of tea."

Ida beamed. "A thousand blessings on you and yours," she said, and smiled when she saw the puzzled look on the other woman's face. "I really needed some tea. Thank you."

Behind her, a familiar voice was speaking. Japie van Reenen. She put her head down and stayed very still.

"You haven't listened to a word I've said." He spoke in a loud whisper.

Silence.

"Rene? Speak to me."

Ida tilted her head and eyed him above the rim of her cup.

The man sat at the table, his large body making the table look child-sized. He bent forward, covering most of the available space at the table. Sitting opposite him was Rene. With her back rammed up against the back of the chair, she faced away from her husband. Ida had never seen her look like this before. Her gaze fixed on the cold-drink dispenser. For someone usually so in control, she looked like an over-heating geyser.

"Rene," Japie lowered his voice. "Are you listening to me?"

Rene suddenly leaned forward and hissed loud enough for Ida to hear. "Japie van Reenen, in all the years we've been married, I have tried to be a good wife. I have made excuses for your rudeness and temper–'you're under pressure' or 'you're tired.' But these last few days, it's like I've had laser surgery and I can see you properly for the first time. Sometimes you're just plain mean."

"Rene, wha…?"

She jabbed a well manicured finger across the table at him, "No. You listen." She hesitated a second then continued. "Japie, I don't think I can take any more."

Japie's eyes grew cold. "What are you going to do? Go back to mama?"

Rene sat still for a few seconds staring at her husband then bent down and snapped up her handbag from the floor next to her. She placed her empty cup carefully on the table and without another look at him left the cafeteria.

Ida found herself openly staring at her neighbors. So much for 'having it all.' She'd always thought Rene was so lucky, having a husband (albeit an angry one), a beautiful home and fashionable clothes—not to mention a stunning body. Then, of course, there was little Estelle. Ida hadn't been envious, but she had been intimidated by the perfection of this woman's life.

It was all a myth.

She quietly unhitched her handbag from the back of her chair, grasped her tea in her other hand and turned her head away in an attempt to keep Japie from recognizing her. She snuck out the cafeteria after Rene. On reaching the corridor to the wards, and hoping Japie hadn't seen her, she hurried after her neighbor.

Ahead, Rene took the route to the children's ward.

Ida increased her pace.

Rene turned around, saw Ida, and slipped into a courtyard.

Ida followed. She found Rene pressed against the glass of the enclosure.

"Rene?" She said quietly from the doorway. "I know it's none of my business but I can see you're going through a hard time. Is there anything I can do for you?"

Rene's now-open face stared back at her. The fire in her had gone out like a damp squib. The stiffness in her shoulders crumbled and sagged until Ida thought she'd collapse in front of her. Ida moved around next to Rene and placed an arm around her and drew her in. When she felt no resistance she found herself hugging her warmly. And the woman whom Ida had admired and held in awe for so long... sobbed in her arms.

Finally, Ida led Rene to the bench and helped her sit down. While Ida listened, the whole story came out. Estelle's snake bite. Japie's anger and control. The loneliness. The emptiness of a marriage where partnership was not an option. As she took it all in, Ida felt a sneaking sense of gratitude creep in as she began to realize just how much she'd had with Tony. They'd had their moments, but she always knew he loved her. They were a team.

Rene's head dropped into her hands. "What do I do?"

Ida realized Rene wasn't speaking to her. She waited.

"Where do I go?" She glanced up at Ida. "I can't go back to that."

Ida placed a hand on her knee. "Rene, whatever you do, don't make any hasty decisions. You need to talk to someone who can help you." The thought seemed to settle Rene.

"You know Ida, I have never told anyone what I've told you and I don't know you well. My mother doesn't even know." She looked concerned. "You won't mention this to anyone, will you?"

"I'm glad I could be here for you. And of course I won't say anything."

Rene suddenly seemed to realize something. "Ida, why are you here?"

"It's a long story." Ida searched Rene's face to discern how much to tell her.

"I'm fine. It will be good for me to think about something else."

So, very briefly, Ida told of the incidents that had brought her there. The children living without parents. The rape of the girls. She concluded, "The doctor's just told me the little boy, Surprise, has AIDS." She felt her eye's prickle with tears.

Rene stared at her. "I don't know what to say. I knew the AIDS problem was bad but I didn't imagine how it might affect children."

"Me too."

"I couldn't have done what you did."

"I didn't think I could either. It's amazing what you can do for others that you can't do for yourself."

"What's going to happen to the children?"

"I don't know."

"You've come this far. I'm sure you'll work it out." Rene glanced at her watch. "I need to go. I don't know what I can do but if you need help, please call me." She lay her hands on Ida's shoulder. "If you hadn't come to speak to me today, I hate to think what I might have done. Thank you."

"I'm glad I was here." Ida smiled. "It worked for both of us."

CHAPTER 18

The man lay in bed listening to the waking sounds of dawn. Beside him lay the vibrating body of his wife as she strangled the peace of daybreak with her snoring. What would happen if he brought in that rooster that was competing for ear-time next door, and put it next to his wife? Who would win the noise-war? He suspected the rooster didn't stand a chance.

He crept out of bed and padded over to the window where the world outside was slowly coming into focus with the approaching light. Tomorrow was full moon. This time tomorrow he would be counting his blessings: a few hundred blue ones. A full day's work lay ahead of him so nothing had better go wrong. But, what was he afraid of? The children weren't going anywhere.

The snores swelled to a crescendo followed by a few suspended seconds of silence. Then, throttled sounds, as his wife fought to breathe before the sudden resumption of the snoring. It was the pattern of the night. The pattern of his life. He lived for the silences.

This was the moment she was most likely to wake up. He seized the pile of clothes lying on the chest of drawers and fled into the sitting room, closing the bedroom door quietly behind him.

He headed over to the doorway of the tiny room behind the red couch and peered in. Weak rays of sun revealed the sleeping forms of the children. Twelve-year-old Benson, second born, lay sprawled across the top of the bed while his younger cousin, Sifiso slept at the foot of the bed. A single blanket lay crumpled between them, not covering either of them. Jammed between the boys' bed and the wall, a thin foam mattress held the sleeping forms of his other brother's twin sons curled together.

The man shook his head. The last funeral had cost him a whole month's salary. Now both his brothers had gone. Well, he wasn't going. He wasn't stupid. He thumped the side of the doorway.

Benson stirred. "*Baba*, Father?"

The man started. No, Benson. This is my time. "It is not five o'clock yet," he whispered through the door then pulled it closed behind him. At the window he leaned against the sill and pressed his forehead against the cool glass. His eyes closed to the first rays of emerging sun.

The dung beetles were the answer, of course. They filled his wallet. As he thought about it, he thanked his ancestors for showing him where the children lived. Things had been more bearable since he'd found them. And he'd made some important friends. Men who were willing to pay well—everyone knew children didn't give you AIDS.

He wondered again if he should involve his first born, Alfred, in his newest business venture. But, as his thoughts always ended up, it would cut his profit margins, and he wasn't sure if he was ready for that yet. Maybe one day.

Then, without invitation, into his mind came the scene from yesterday's meltdown. What had happened? He'd always prided himself on being the master of control. Except, of course, over the woman.

It scared him.

His first lesson in gaining personal power had been that first night alone in that building where he'd found himself at the end of his run. The church. He'd jammed a bench up against the door then lain down to sleep when he heard the padding of footsteps outside the door. The footsteps stopped. Heavy breathing and a foul smell wafted through the cracks in the planks. Then the scratching began. Whoever, whatever was at the door wanted in… badly.

Where he got the courage or the idea, he didn't know. He began to growl. A low warning growl. He listened. The scratching stopped. Interesting.

The scratching resumed, less confident this time. He growled again, adding intensity to his voice. Once more the scraping stopped. He let out a final, full-blooded snarl. There was a yelp and the would-be intruder disappeared into the night.

In that moment a spark ignited in him. He realized that size did not dictate power, but will. And perceived power had the same effect as real power. But there was danger in remembering. Power, whatever kind, walked hand in hand with constant anxiety, because he knew the truth: he was just a child.

He had to stop going back like this. Some of the walls he'd been so careful to build in his mind were starting to strain. Ancient pain was bleeding through the ever-widening gaps in his armor and he didn't know how to stop it.

He needed to remember the good parts. There was Sifiso, the Hat Man. One year older than he was and half his size. They'd met at the rubbish dump two days into his new life.

The truck had just dumped a load of bulging black bags on the outskirts of the dump, when out of nowhere, a small group of people materialized. The race to find food began. He soon realized there was a pecking order here at the dump. If you found food that had no maggots yet or other treasures like discarded clothes, you surreptitiously slipped them under your shirt and continued as though you hadn't found anything, or the bully of the bunch would descend on you and relieve you of your plunder.

His treasure that day was two crusts of white bread still enclosed in the plastic packet that read, "Brown's Bread. Stays fresh as the day it was made." A diminutive boy with a lop-sided smile sidled up to him.

"I will share my avocado with you if you give me one of those pieces of bread." He spoke out of the side of his mouth, his body bent over as he picked through the mush of garbage. When he straightened, he adjusted the three hats that were jammed one on top of the other on his head. "I am the Hat Man. If you want to be my friend you will never touch my hats."

The strange boy thought for a moment then seemed to make a decision. He pointed to the hats. "These are my friends. This top hat protects my plans. The middle one my power. And this one," his skinny finger jabbed at a wide brimmed felt, "my stomach."

He was crazy, but when introductions were over the two boys became inseparable. To Hat Man, life was a game played between him on one side and everyone else on the other. He wrote the rule book and changed the rules according to the whim of one of his hats.

Though tiny for his age, Hat Man had spunk and a spark of mischief. As a result, by the time a year had gone by, both boys had developed certain talents directly related to Hat Man's lunatic personality. The first was running. This one was the easiest to develop as the people who chased them mostly had old legs. The second was creating strategies to ease people away from their most desirable goods, especially food.

The man sighed at the memory and the ache inside grew. They were just two orphaned runts in an unfriendly world. No, it wasn't all bad. You got used to holding your breath as you bit into rotting food and it wasn't long before you discovered eating the odd maggot didn't kill you.

And, like the sun breaking through the clouds on a stormy day, something good sometimes happened to make their lives brighter. Finding a blanket someone had dropped along the path to the dump was one of those times. How often had he and Hat Man huddled together under it in the winter months while the wind whined through the roofless ruin of a house they lived in? If they tucked themselves into the corner, furthest away from the crumbling doorway, it kept the sting of the cold from reaching them.

And the day they found a plastic packet of uneaten sandwiches which someone had discarded after a party? They ate until their bellies ballooned over their shorts—then promptly were sick. Sick, yes, but oh it was good. That day, Hat Man took down his stomach hat and ran his fingers around the rim. "Thank you," he whispered, then slipped it back on.

Three years later Hat Man buried his hats. He no longer needed them. He had a real friend. The man sighed again. He was my only friend.

Now, outside his house, the sun had appeared above the horizon but hid behind a dark cloud. He heard movement in his bedroom. Life was strange. After all he'd been through, all the experiences that taught him about people and life, it was like he'd married his mother.

When he first met his wife, she spoke softly and little, but one week into the marriage the real woman appeared–shrieking and cursing and telling him how to run his life. She had 'boss-itis.' But he was patient. One day, and it was coming soon, he would let her know who the boss really was.

It was difficult living with Mrs. Boss, but he had decided he would never treat his children the way he'd been treated. Fortunately, she took it out on him and not so much on the children, but there comes a time in every man's life when he has to do what he has to do.

He'd been lucky that first night in the church. The pastor had found him asleep when he arrived for church the next day. He finally told the pastor what had happened to him and had been offered a place to live. It was tempting to go and live with a normal family and not to have to think about finding food but cruel memories of home propelled him away from accepting.

Sometimes though, in his quiet times, he wished he'd accepted the pastor's offer. He was a good man. The best part was that the pastor had put him through school. Now that he, himself, was a man, he realized the pastor was very poor and it must have cost him to send a stray boy to school. One day he would find the pastor and say thank you.

CHAPTER 19

Ida found herself humming. When was the last time? For the first time, she was beginning to understand what Mom always said: when you build a wall around you to keep out the hurt, you keep out joy as well. But the wall was collapsing and she felt a fresh stream of pleasure flowing in. If Surprise came home today, they were going to party. It would have to be a low-budget fun time but tonight they were celebrating. She, Ida Morgan, was officially coming out of mourning.

As Ida arrived at the nurse's station, the nurse of a thousand smiles looked up from her paper work.

"Good morning, Mrs. Morgan," she said.

Ida smiled back. "Hello, Nurse Bokaba. Has the doctor seen Surprise yet?"

"You can take him home. He's waiting for you."

Ida could have hugged her. She hurried into the ward. Next to the bed, a nurse she hadn't seen before cleared the breakfast tray while she chatted to the boy. For a moment Ida stood and watched. Surprise sat in bed, his face lifted to the nurse and grinning.

"Hi, Surprise." She waited at the doorway.

"*Mama*." He tried to jump off the bed to get to her.

She ran over to him and pulled him into her arms. "My special boy." He held on tight. After a while she felt the nurse's gentle touch. A clean tissue appeared around her arm. The nurse laughed.

Surprise pulled away from her. "Where is Busi?"

"She is at home waiting for you."

"I want to go home."

"Mrs. Morgan," the nurse said from the doorway. "Nurse Bophiso will inform you about Surprise's medication; then you can get it from the dispensary. I will help Surprise get dressed and he will be waiting for you."

That all done, Surprise sat on Ida's lap at the entrance to the clinic while they waited for Shell to arrive. Absentmindedly, Ida watched the boy clutch the bag of medication close to his body. Her arms tightened around him, her mind going in circles, thinking of the rigorous routine of medication. What if she forgot something? His life depended on it. Was she up to this? Her head snapped up. It appeared she'd made some subconscious decisions about Surprise's future.

Shelly appeared at the entrance and flung herself through the door. While one hand attempted to bring order to her ruffled hair, the other gripped her handbag and reached up for the car keys dangling from her mouth. She stopped short when she saw Surprise. "Hhhrga." She took the keys out her mouth and tried again, "Hey. And who is this?"

Surprise tightened his grip on the packet.

Ida whispered in his ear. "*Sawubona, Mama* Link."

He closed his eyes and pressed against Ida.

"He's not used to the paler variety of humans," Ida said.

Shelly laughed. "Let's go. I'm dying to hear all your news." She scrutinized Ida's face. "You really did all that... stuff?"

Ida nodded, picked up Surprise and followed Shelly to her white Pathfinder. "How much time do you have, Shell?"

"I've cleared most of my day. Where do we go first?"

"Home, James." She had a thought. "Shelly, my car is stuck in Masoyi. Do you think we could ask Grant to help me get it out?"

Shelly pushed the key in the ignition. "If I can get him out of bed. A friend of his spent the night. They were up half the night playing video games. I can't wait for school to start again. Sometimes I wish I could go to sleep until he is 30." She chuckled when she saw Ida's face. "He has as much desire for work as a drugged slug. I long for the day I can let go the cattle prod to motivate him–metaphorically speaking," she added quickly.

Shelly switched off the engine, leaned over to the dashboard and pulled out her cell phone and dialed. She waited. "Wake up. Wake up." She sang into the phone. Her tapping on the steering wheel intensified. While she waited, she noticed Ida trying to get her attention.

"Do you have a jack in your car?" Ida mouthed.

Shell nodded. Then, "Oh, hi. It's me." She raised her eyes to Ida. "Mrs. Morgan needs you and Brian to help her get her car out of Masoyi. Can you come and help us? No. Not tomorrow, right now. In about half an hour?" Her head bounced around as she waited for him to speak. "I know its the holidays but Mrs. Morgan really needs you. Okay. We'll be there soon." She clicked off and restarted the engine. "We're set to go."

Driving through Ida's gate, Shelly stopped the car and stared. "I thought you said there were nine children? I see a few million."

Ida searched through the sea of children. "Three of them must be Mrs. Nkosi's children. It's hard to see exactly." The moving mass of rambunctious children chased each other around the garden, or sparred together. Then almost as one, they seemed to notice the two women in the car. They stopped and stared.

Ida rolled down her window and waved. The brief wall of stillness broke. Bandile, Samson and Promise rushed over to Ida's side of the car, yelling.

Behind them, Moses followed shyly. She peered through the back window of the car and screamed. The door flew open and she pulled Surprise out in a great bear-hug. She spun him around, dancing and laughing, pulling the rest of the children in, all pushing and shoving and shouting.

"Ida," Shelly bent her head to examine Ida's face, "I haven't seen you look this happy for a very long time."

Ida just grinned. She lifted her head to see Mrs. Nkosi standing at the kitchen door. She hauled herself out the car and hurried over to her neighbor.

"Mrs. Nkosi. How can I say thank you for all you've done?" Ida rested her hand on the woman's arm.

"I am glad I can help you. The children they are very good. My children are happy they have some friends to play with."

Ten minutes later, Mrs. Nkosi left with her children. Ida waved goodbye and was turning to go inside when her eye caught a movement under the yellow bush growing at the corner of her house. "Cricket." She ran over to the bemused cat hiding from the noise and laughter. "You're back." Cricket allowed himself to be cuddled for exactly three seconds then jumped out of Ida's arms and made a bee-line for the kitchen. So much for love being stronger than food!

The cat fed, Moses was once more put in charge with instructions on how to keep the children occupied.

Before she left with Shelly, Ida retrieved several blocks of firewood of varying sizes from the pile in the garage and threw them into the trunk of Shelly's car. The two women set off.

When they arrived at Shelly's house, at the corner of Jacaranda Drive, they waited for Grant and Brian. The sudden sound of children's laughter made Ida jump. She looked around her. Who?

Where? Shelly picked up her phone and put it to her ear.

Ida giggled. "That's some ring tone, Shelly," Ida said when her friend had finished her call.

"*Ja.* I love it. Children's laughter is my favorite sound."

Grant ran down the steps to the car, followed by two other teens. All three youths piled in. "Jonathan said he would help too," Grant said. There were introductions all round, then the boys went back to heckling each other over which rugby team was going to win the Currie Cup. Two were in favor of the Bulls. One for the Sharks.

Done with the verbal sparring, Grant suddenly sat forward in his seat and spoke to Ida. "What happened to your car, Mrs. M?" Grant asked.

Ida explained briefly what had happened. At first, the teens were quiet, but then came a barrage of questions. Where did the children get food? Why didn't someone help them? How could they live by themselves?

They were the same questions Ida had been asking herself just days before. She answered as best she could.

"I have lived here all of my life and I never knew something like this could happen so close to me," Shelly said, her voice quiet.

"The doctor told me there could be up to two million orphans in South Africa," Ida said.

"Wow. The whole population in South Africa is only about 49 million," Brian said. The boys chatted together in the back seat. Ida was surprised at the interest this conversation was generating. Two major cultures lived side by side and there was still so little real knowledge and understanding of each other.

Approaching Masoyi, Ida began to feel the energy of the moment drain from her. What if the chicken man wasn't there today? Would she remember which road to take? Would the angry mob still be there? Judging from the burnt out shell of a Camry on the side of the road, and the scattered rocks and debris still strewn across it, this was where it had all happened the other night.

Finally, there he was. The chicken man. She sank back into her seat. "Turn left after the chicken man," she said to Shelly, who slowed down and pulled over to the side of the road.

"You're joking, right? There's no road."

"Not what we're used to, hey?" Ida asked. "Turn left here."

"I'm not going up there. What if my car breaks down? What if we get stuck?"

"You can do it, Mom." Grant patted his mother on the shoulder. Shelly eased her Pathfinder onto the dirt track and they began their torturous journey up the hill.

Halfway up the hill, Shelly took her gaze off the trail for a moment to look at Ida. "You're sure this is the right way?" Ida nodded and they continued upward.

Cresting the hill that led to the graveyard, they heard the mournful wail of singing through the open windows of the car. At the edge of the cemetery, under trees in the far corner, two groups of people swayed in time to their songs, stamping and singing. The group nearest them was close enough for them to observe a small wooden box around which the mourners gathered.

Shelly stopped the car and switched off the engine. Silently they watched a woman fling herself onto the child's coffin, releasing a piercing howl above the collective sound of the mourners.

A whispered 'shame' came over the back of the car. Two of the boys dropped their gaze and looked at anything but the scene outside. Grant sat with his head pressed hard against the headrest, his eyes wide and staring. No playful chatter.

Shelly turned the key and eased the gearshift into first and inched past. None of the mourners took any interest in the car. Slowly, the windows closed to shut out the distressing expressions of grief, but what the windows shut out, the heart couldn't. Each one was silent. The car bounced over the hill and down the other side.

Ida forced her thoughts back to what she was doing. Was it still there? She held her breath. There it was. Still in one piece and stuck in the hole. "Thank goodness," she said aloud. "Nothing's been…"

"Looks like the right front tire is missing," came Grant's voice from the back of the car. Ida strained to see. Then she saw it. The right front bumper rested on the rock. "It's been stolen." She swung open the door, barely waiting for the Pathfinder to come to a stop. She ran to the driver's side of the car. "They've damaged the lock trying to open the door." She hurried to the passenger side. "This side's okay. They've only taken one tire. We can use the spare in the trunk." She removed the keys from her handbag.

Grant reached her side and stretched out his hand to take them from her. "We'll do it." The boys took over. While they worked, unusually quiet, Ida stared at the little grey houses down the hill. Some of her worst and some of her most memorable experiences had happened down there. Thank goodness she didn't have to go back. Just a few days ago she'd thought her world had come to an end. Now, looking back, her life had only just begun. When the memories became uncomfortable she turned to find Shelly waiting silently next to her.

"That's where I found them." She pointed down the hill.

"I don't know how you did it," Shelly said, shaking her head.

"If you'd met those little people, you would have done the same."

"Mrs. M, the tire's on." Grant's shout ended the conversation.

She watched him yank at the jack handle. Slowly the car came to rest on the ground. "Thanks, Grant. When you're finished would you take the jack round to the other side where the tire is stuck in the hole then raise the car on that side?" She moved over to Shelly's car, removed the packet of firewood, and took it over to where the two boys were easing the jack into its socket. "As soon as the wheel clears the hole, we'll fill it with chunks of wood."

"I'll do it." Brian took the wood from Ida. It worked. Grant lowered the car. Then Ida, holding a deep breath, drove carefully off the rock. Yes! Another frustration dealt with and her independence restored. She wound down her window and shouted her thanks to Shelly and the boys.

"We'll drive behind you to make sure you get back onto the road safely," Shelly said as she and the boys hopped into their car.

"Thanks. Hey, why don't you guys come and meet the children sometime?" Ida asked.

Grant leaned out the window. "Do they know how to play cricket?"

"They're quick learners." She turned to her friend. "Shelly, you've been an angel. Thanks."

Ida pushed the gear-lever into first. Thankfully, there was nothing seriously wrong with the car. She cleared the top of the hill just as an old VW Beetle appeared in a cloud of dust coming from the other direction. The dust enveloped the mourners who stood watching two men shovel a mound of earth back into the open grave.

The VW wobbled from side to side. Ida would have thought

nothing of it had the driver not screeched to a halt just before the track descended down to the children's house and flung his arm up in front of his face. She couldn't see his face. Did he get a fright or was he hiding something? Not that she cared, of course. She shook her head. Not surprising that there was a nasty crack in the VW's windscreen with that kind of driving.

Ida headed down the track to the main road. First stop–to buy a new tire. Hopefully Wheel Base would let her pay for it at the end of the month.

CHAPTER 20

The man sat in his car, shaking. That was close. Was that driver coming up from the children's area? Quick, get the number plate. He turned round to see. He peered through the back window. DH...4... was it 3 or 8? He slammed his hand on the steering wheel. Maybe he should go after the Mazda. Check it out. No, too risky.

Was someone interested in the children? *Cha. Hhayi*, he was imagining things. It was probably just a coincidence. Why would the car be coming from the direction of the dung beetles' house? Nah. But then, maybe... was he running into trouble?

Just in case, he should be doubly careful. He sat there tossing around his options: to check on the children now, or not to. He started up his car.

CHAPTER 21

Arriving home at last, Ida wondered for the 100th time what had happened to Simeon. He would never just disappear without telling her. She tried him again on her landline but his phone just rang. Maybe the police had had more luck. She phoned Sergeant Jawena. No, there was no sign of Simeon.

"Have you tried the hospitals?" she asked. There was a pause on the other end of the line. "Themba Hospital? It's the closest."

She heard the policeman sigh. "I have phoned the hospital but I will try again." He hung up. Poor man. He was doing his best.

Was nothing easy about all this? Into her mind came a picture of a small dilapidated brick house where, while she sat in her nice kitchen on a comfortable chair, a man lay on soiled rags, waiting to die.

She had to do something. She pulled out the Mpumalanga phone book. *Goedgenoeg Plaas*. No listing. 'Good Enough Farm'? Nothing. She should have asked for the farmer's name. What was it the man said? Something about working with the chickens? It clicked. 'Buy and Save' sold eggs with the logo of a farmer holding up an egg and a caption which started with the word *"Goedgenoeg"* It was a long shot. She dialed Jako Cronje. "Hi, Jako. It's Ida. Listen. Who do 'Buy and Save' get their eggs from?"

"I'm just with a customer. Give me a sec and I'll find out. I'll phone you back." Her phone rang a few minutes later. "It's *Goedgenoeg Hoenders*. 'Good Enough Chickens.'"

That was it. Ida remembered the byline: *"Goedgenoeg hoenders is goedgenoeg vir almal.* Good enough chickens are good enough for everyone." That was it. She thanked Jako and looked up the number.

A man answered on the first ring. "Hello. Henk here."

After introducing herself, she said, "It's a long story but I wanted to tell you about a man on your property who is dying of AIDS. His father is old and can't take care of him properly. Is there…"

"Ma'am, I don't mean to be rude but the people on my farm know where to go to the clinic."

"I understand but this man is too sick to move. He needs help."

There was silence on the other end. "If he's that bad, even the hospitals send them home to die."

"You won't help him?" Ida tried to keep the bitterness from her voice.

"Ma'am, I have 150 people working for me. Their families live on my farm. I feed them. I don't have the time to chase after every sick person. They got this disease from all their nonsense with women. Now they want me to help them?"

Ida chose not to react. "If I can find someone to come and help him, would that be okay?"

"Just let the guard at the gate know why they are coming."

Ida replaced the phone slowly and breathed deeply. She slumped down on the kitchen chair. Who could she call to help? The figure of Thomas entered her mind. Tall and emaciated, a skeleton dressed in skin—yet he was on the road to a longer life because a nurse from Acts Clinic heard about him. She cared for him in his shack, giving him retrovirals and a reason to live. Ida used to see him each Sunday, sitting in the front row of her small restaurant church, beaming.

She phoned the clinic and they said they would send someone to him as soon as they could. With her heart feeling lighter she took a cup of tea into the lounge and peered through the open window at the children playing outside. A rag-tangle of happiness.

Three of the boys scattered in front of Bandile as he chased after them, his grin exposing the bloodthirstiness of the hunt. They all twisted and turned to evade him except for the little guy. Surprise stood waiting for his brother with face upturned, his mouth wide in anticipation. Bandile rushed at him, clapping his hands. "Run Surprise. Run." At the last moment, Surprise stepped aside. Bandile flashed past and slapped straight into Samson, with a breath-emptying grunt.

Ida's eyes clamped tight. When she looked up again, the two older boys lay on the lawn chests heaving and rubbing their foreheads. Phineas looked on, laughing, while Surprise inched up to Bandile. "Sorry. Sorry."

Bandile sat up suddenly and faced Surprise with an oversized frown on his face. "Grrr..." He rose to his feet slowly, his arms raised menacingly above his head. Ramming giant footsteps into the grass, he set off after his little brother. Surprise shrieked and set off, his little bird-legs stamping across the lawn.

Ida watched her boys. That was it: her boys. Any lingering doubts she'd had were ice cubes under boiling water. These two boys and their sister were as much part of her as her appendix. But what about the other children? Her limited resources wouldn't stretch that far. She needed to find homes for them. Now was as good a time as any.

She looked up Social Services and dialed. A Mrs. Vilakazi answered.

"Mrs. Morgan," she said, after hearing Ida's story, "there are almost one million orphans in Mpumalanga alone and very few social workers. There are maybe a couple of thousand children for every social worker."

"That's appalling. How long will it take to help them? What am I supposed to do?"

"We need all the information we can get about the extended families of the children." Ida could hear the woman trying to be patient. "Do they have any aunts, uncles or grandmothers? Are any of them prepared to take them? After that, they need to be assessed."

"Two of the boys have been living in a house with nothing in it except a couple of blankets. All their stuff was taken by an uncle. They mustn't go to that uncle."

"Mrs. Morgan, why don't you find out what you can and then send me all the information? I'll see what I can do. Oh, and Mrs. Morgan, there are organizations in the communities who may be able to help you. Like 'Hands at Work.'"

Ida knew the organization. She could always ask them. She put down the phone. What chance did the children have in the chaos of such an overworked and seriously understaffed social welfare system?

She hurried outside to speak with Promise. "Come for a walk with me." Ida said when she found her. She took the child's hand and looked into her smiling face. Together they wandered to the rockery in the back garden and sat on a large smooth rock. She came straight to the point.

"Promise," she said, "do you have any uncles or aunties who live near you?"

"*Yebo.*" Affirmative.

"Would you like to go and live with them?"

The smile faded and her head lowered.

Ida tried again. "Do you know where they live?"

No response.

"Promise?"

The child nodded.

"Why don't you want to go to them?" Ida leaned forward and gently lifted the child's chin so she could see into her eyes. But Promise gazed at her feet.

"Did they hurt you?"

Still she said nothing.

"Speak to me." She moved close to Promise and slid her arm around her shoulder.

Promise sighed. "We live with them, but we run away." When Ida said nothing, she continued. "I must work for my auntie. Clean everything in the house. And I must cook and look after my sisters and my auntie's baby. There is not enough food and I am too tired." Just as Ida thought she'd finished, Promise continued. "The boys they chase me and I can't do my work. Then my auntie is angry because the work is not done. She beat me."

Ida rose and kicked at the border of bricks around the rock garden. She felt heat rise in her chest and up into her face. Plastic bags seemed to have more value than these children... "Use them up. Throw them out." Their past was irrelevant; in the present they were invisible and they had no future. She breathed in deeply and tried to hide her negativity from Promise.

"I won't let you go back to them." She turned to face the child. "Do you have any other family?"

"My mother's sister. But she got six children. Four of them is the children of her brother."

"What about your father's family?"

"They live in Swaziland." Promise plucked a Barberton daisy and tugged at the circle of red petals.

Watch it—porcupine backing in. What if she wasn't able to find any suitable relatives? If she worked hard, she could keep Moses, Bandile, and Surprise. But what of the others? And if she found relatives, would they be loved and cared for? She was beginning to doubt that, too. If *she* was losing hope with all *she* had, how could these children possibly still remain positive when they had nothing?

Just then she heard the phone ring in the house. "Wait for me. I'll be back in a minute." She rushed inside and snatched up the phone.

Mrs. Nkosi greeted her. "My husband and I were talking. We wondered if you knew anything about the little girl who is with you?"

Which one? "Goodness?"

"Yes, the one who came without brothers and sisters."

Ida felt her heart beating faster. "It seems she has no family. She was working for a woman for food but the woman fired her for not being strong enough." She had a thought. "Mrs. Nkosi, may I ask why you're asking?"

"Three years ago we had a baby girl. She got dysentery and she died. We thought... we thought maybe we should take Goodness to be a sister for our three boys."

Ida felt a stab of adrenaline shoot into her. "Really? You'd be willing to take her?"

"We are thinking about it. We will speak to you when we have talked some more." They ended the call.

Finally, good news. It was way too early to get excited but... "Yaah!" Ida yelled. One down, five more to go. Maybe. She skipped outside to continue her conversation with Promise.

CHAPTER 22

Right now, Ida had to work through some troubling thoughts which had been nagging at her. She had a difficult conversation coming up and she needed to work out how she should deal with it. Where should she start?

Ida opened the lounge door and stepped outside. She breathed in the delicate aroma of jasmine growing against the side of the house. Through the wire fence around the perimeter of her garden she gazed on a stricken wild fig. A week ago it had been a magnificent specimen of a tree. Now, its immense branches trailed helplessly through the water. Over the years she and Tony had lived here, this tree had become a symbol of strength and permanence. Now it was neither. Termites would do to it what they did best, and time and the weather would complete their responsibility to the cycle of life.

Ida returned to the rock where she and Promise had sat earlier and lowered herself onto it. She squared her shoulders and prepared herself for what she was about to say. The more she thought about it, the more she realized she really had only one question. Why?

"God, why did you let Tony die? You could have saved him, but you didn't. I just want to know why?" The only answer was the rush of the stream nearby and the children playing in the front garden.

"Are you listening, Lord? I'm split in two like that wild fig over there. Half of me is dead." From deep inside her stomach she felt the pain rise and she knew there was no device to stop the volcano erupting. She jumped up and ran into her bedroom, threw herself onto her bed and buried her face in the pillow. She howled it all up.

As the tears subsided, a familiar track appeared in her mind and she knew she was about to jump onto it. Again. Going round and round with the same old questions, following the same circular rut. Chasing the same thoughts and getting the same answer. Silence. And the rut grew deeper and deeper.

How could she pull herself away from the track's compulsion? What was really going on inside her? Her thoughts leapt back to the day at the river with the youths. Maybe she needed to find a different question here too.

Okay, she needed to search from another perspective. When Tony disappeared from her life, she felt God had too. What if her pain was so loud it had drowned out God's voice? When the music of his presence was silenced, maybe she thought he'd left her as well.

Or did she, deep down, feel God was punishing her by allowing Tony to die? What was the truth? The children had lost far more than she had yet she knew without doubt that God loved them. Even in their aloneness, he'd never abandoned them. They hadn't deserved their lives nor had they done anything wrong. Then, out of the fog of uncertainty, she knew. The question she'd really been asking was 'Lord, do you still care about me? I don't feel you, I can't hear you. Do you still love me?'

She lay back, tucked her feet up close against her body. Empty. Her inner monologue was still. That was when she heard it: an urging in her spirit.

"I loved you before Tony died and I love you now." The wind whispered through the trees outside. "I was with you before Tony died and I'm with you now." A pause. "I never change."

"But Lord, how can you say you love me after all that's happened?" She listened.

"I died for you."

Like the right puzzle piece falling into place, she knew it was true.

Into her mind came the words of an old song she used to sing. She hurried over to the piano, stretched out her fingers and coaxed out the almost forgotten tune. Sweet notes of singing filled the room. "He didn't come to judge the world or take away man's choice; eradicate all consequence or silence mankind's voice. He came to heal our brokenness; bring freedom from all doubt. Forgive and clean the blackest heart; transform from inside-out." When she finished she sat back and felt the peace of God seep into the cracks and brokenness of her heart.

CHAPTER 23

Ida sat at the piano, feeling like a fish eagle released from captivity into the immense sky of possibilities. She'd lived so long in the greyness of uncertainty; knowing, but not really believing. Now, her churning thoughts lay at rest.

"*Mama*?"

Ida looked up with a start. Moses stood at the door, a shy grin on her face. For several seconds, Ida's thoughts hung suspended in space. She stared at Moses.

"What did you say?"

"*Mama*." The grin was back. Moses looked down.

Ida dashed over to the child, grabbed her round her waist and whirled her round and round until lightheadedness flung them both onto the carpet in a laughing, crying heap. She folded her arms around the girl, eyes scrunched tight. "You can speak."

"*Yebo*, Mama."

It was Ida's turn to be speechless. "Can you tell me what happened? Why did you stop speaking?"

Moses' hands dropped to the floor. Ida pulled her gently to the couch where they sat together. Finally, Moses began to talk.

"When the men come, the first time," she raised a finger to show Ida, "the big man, he grab me. I try to run away. He put his hand here," she indicated her throat. "He say, 'If you run away I will kill your brothers.'" Her mouth began to tremble. "He say, 'If you tell someone I will cut your throat.'" She sank back into the couch and covered her face.

"Do you know his name? What did he look like?"

"He wear sunglasses and a big hat."

"He is tall? Fat?"

"No. No. He is thin like a stick but he is taller than you." That's fortunate. "After that, he never come down the hill again. He send men to come down to us. The boys they are too small, they cannot help us."

"Do you know any of the men?"

"No. They is never the same."

Ida held onto her tightly, saying with clenched teeth. "They will *never* hurt you again."

Moses broke away from Ida's hug. "When he do this," she said looking at Ida through her tears. "I tell myself if I speak he will hurt my brothers. So I never speak again."

"What changed your mind?"

"My brothers they are safe. You are *Mama* to us. Now I can speak."

"Yes, I am your *Mama* and I will help you." She thought for a moment. Should she ask? "Moses, tell me about your family?"

Moses leaned into Ida. "My *Mama* she is very kind. She look after us when my father work. He only come home sometimes. Sometimes Saturday. Sometimes Sunday. When Surprise is baby we not see my father for a long time. One day he come home. He look like this." She held up her thin pinky finger. "I hear him shout to my mother. She hide behind the house and I hear her cry. She not tell me what is wrong."

For a moment, Moses disappeared into her thoughts. Ida waited for her to continue.

"My father he stay at home. He is sick. My mother work very hard. She help him. But there is no food. Bandile and Surprise, they cry. Sometimes I cry but not when my mother is there." She stared out the window. "Sometimes I help woman at the river to carry water. They give me twenty cents. Sometimes they cannot give me money."

"What about school?"

"I cannot go to school. I have no money. One day I come home and my mother is crying. Many people is there. They is crying. My father is dead. They take my father away. He is bury in the ground."

"When my father die, my mother she work for chicken farm. It is good. We eat pap when she come home at night. Sometimes she bring a piece of chicken and give it to us. But I can see my mother is get like my father." The little finger came out again. "My mother she is sick."

Ida felt Moses' body wilt next to her. "You can tell me another time," she said.

The child lifted her head. "It is okay." She straightened. "Now I am *Mama*. I must clean her and help her. She cannot move. She is heavy for me."

For several seconds Ida waited and when Moses spoke, Ida could only just hear her.

"She smile at me. She say I am a good girl."

Ida turned her face away so Moses couldn't see the tears.

"When the men come to bury *Mama*, I have no money to give them. They say is okay but they put her in small box. It is not new one." She rubbed her eyes as if trying to rub out the memory. "I want my *Mama* but she is gone. Then the men come."

The two of them sat side by side thinking their own thoughts.

Could she ask Moses? There were a few things she was dying to find out. "I have two questions I want to ask you, Moses, but if you don't want to answer them, it's okay."

Moses nodded.

"I heard Samson tell you 'God has ears.' What did he mean?"

"After the mans come the second time and we know they will come again, I say to Samson, 'There is no one to help us. We must ask God. Maybe he will protect us.' He say, 'Busi, does God have ears like you and me?' When he see I am sad, he say, 'You can speak to him if you like.' So I pray to God and ask him to help us with the bad mans."

"And then I came?" Ida said.

Moses nodded. "Now we know God has ears."

More silence. Then, "I have one more question. How did you get to be in the blue box on the river?"

CHAPTER 24

Moses had thought often of the answer to that question. She remembered that day. Every small detail.

Five or six *mamas* and *gogos* were at the stream when she and the boys had arrived. The women stood over their buckets, their arms pumped up and down as they rubbed their washing or slapped wet clothes against the rocks to beat the dirt out. They shouted out their news to each other while the children splashed in the water nearby.

One woman stood out. She greeted Moses and the boys as she always did. She would stop now and then to talk and play with her child when he called out to her from the water's edge. She was the one Moses chose to help so she and the boys could eat that day.

Moses pushed Bandile forward to speak for her. "*Mama,*" he said. "Can we help you? We can take water to your house?" He held up an empty water bottle in his hand to show the woman and then looked up at Moses for approval. Moses nodded.

The woman stopped rubbing her soapy clothes in the big plastic container at her feet and looked up kindly at him. "I have no money." She raised a hand enveloped in foam and swiped it across her forehead, leaving a trail of bubbles along her hair line. "If you wait for me you can come to my house and I will give you some *pap.*"

For a moment Moses was intrigued by the bubbles on the woman's face. How they slowly collapsed, leaving a thin trail of soap scum across her brow. She suddenly realized the woman was waiting for a response. She pressed her hands together in thanks and the woman went back to her washing.

The three of them walked off together. Moses could see by the boys' faces they were excited at the prospect of eating today. In the back of her mind, she thought she would keep a little of the food for the other children. If there was enough. *Pap* became hard and dry when left to cool but it was better than nothing at all.

They found a large area of shade under a bushwillow growing several meters away from the stream's edge. While Bandile and Surprise found sticks to beat the branches of the bush they sheltered under, Moses watched the other children playing in the water.

She lost her sense of time until a small boy ran out of the water, stamping his feet and holding his arms. Even from where she sat, she could see him shivering. Yes, she could feel it too. It was growing cool. She stared up at the darkening sky. They needed to leave before the rain came. As she looked, the sun disappeared behind leaden clouds. At the same moment, bursts of wind blustered and blew around them. Further up-river, she saw the tell-tale signs of a massive thunderstorm. Vertical stripes of black rain-clouds already pummeling the earth. It was only a matter of time before it reached them.

She watched the kind woman empty the last of her rinsing water and place the container at the edge of the stream. She willed her to move more quickly, but the woman had her own rhythm. She left the container and gathered her clean washing that lay spread out over the long grass. She was about to throw it in her blue container when two men appeared.

They stood at a distance, looking relaxed. But one by one the women stopped chatting and turned to scrutinize the strangers.

Moses' body grew rigid. Men didn't come to the stream to wash clothes. Slowly she maneuvered Surprise away from her. Next to her Bandile stiffened as he, too, observed the men. She indicated to Bandile to run as fast as he could and hide with Surprise when she gave the signal. Surprise began to whimper. She gave him a quick hug.

The men's laughter reached them. Then, instead of coming closer, they turned around and started back the way they'd come. The women went back to their tasks in a flurry of activity to get things done before the clouds emptied. But Moses remained vigilant. She jumped up and crept around the edge of the river bed until she came to a bend in the river so she could keep them in sight.

Now she could see them more clearly down a long stretch of sand. She moved behind a bush and waited very still. Sure enough, the men stopped, looked back at the women at the stream, and then parted. The one snuck left, the other right.

Moses knew it was time to go. She'd played this game before and she wasn't getting caught this time. She ran back to Bandile and pushed him away from the stream, steering him to the undergrowth. He took no persuading. She watched her brothers disappear into the bushes. She then ran alongside the river bank moving away from the men. Within seconds she was out of sight of the women.

"Where do you go?" Out of nowhere a large meaty hand gripped her arm. She stared into the face of a man who took up much of the sky in front of her. The wobbling of his fleshy chin scared her more than the grin that failed to reach his eyes. So there was a third man. She'd never seen him before. A spark of defiance blazed in her. She became an angry, spitting cat. She bent her head down, found flesh and ground her teeth into it. The man howled and loosened his grip. Moses shoved hard against him and sped off screaming toward those women who still remained at the water.

Two women came running toward her and stood in front of her. She heard the man cursing. He would reach the bend any moment and see her. The kind woman dumped her container next to the stream, snatched up her washing and indicated Moses should jump in the container. She then threw the damp clothes on top of her. Moses heard her singing.

Inside the container, Moses lay still. She heard loud puffing and wheezing. "Where is the girl?"

"She went there." A woman's voice.

"You lie to me and I will come back to get you." The man must have waddled off.

It started. Great drops of water sporadically smacked the washing that covered Moses. But something was wrong. Apart from the rain, there was silence. Why didn't someone say something? She kept still. Then she heard them. Men's voices. "What have you got in the bucket, *Mama*?" A deep voice, playful, but Moses heard the trap open.

"We think you must share with us," another voice said.

"I must go home now." The voice of the kind woman. "My washing will get too wet." Moses felt the container being nudged closer to the stream. What was the woman doing? What if the container landed in the water? It was an impossible choice. The men, or floating on the scary water when she couldn't swim.

A third voice spoke up. "There is no more time. This will be a bad storm. Give us the girl."

Then they all heard it: a mighty roaring. Growing. Devouring all other sound. "Run!" When the shouting voices had grown quiet, hands reached down and snatched up the washing. "Get out now. The water is coming." But before Moses could raise her head, she felt the container rise and swirl and in an instant she was swept downstream. In all her life, nothing again would ever have the same power to terrify her as this journey she was forced to take.

CHAPTER 25

Today it was Friday. Full moon. The man had a late shift tonight.

He listened for any sounds of his family surfacing for the day. Satisfied everyone was still asleep, he found his cell phone in his jacket pocket and headed down to the banana trees. He wasn't taking any chances. One last glance toward the house. He dialed.

A man answered.

The man recognized the voice. He coughed loudly into the phone, tightening the muscles around his throat so that only a strangled, reedy sound came out. "*Kunjani*? This is…," he looked around him, lowered his voice and gave his name. "I cannot…," cough, "come in today. I have malaria." He listened. "Yes, I must have got it when I visited my mother. No, my shift is 7:00 p.m." He listened. "*Yebo. Ngiyabonga.*" He coughed into the phone. "You will tell the boss?"

He switched it off, straightened up, and strode up to the house. Skirting it and taking the opposite direction of his sleeping wife, he crept around to the front steps and slowly lowered himself onto the top step, stretching himself back against the door. Now, where was he? Today was his day.

He felt very proud. Some people said he'd been lucky. But he knew it was mostly hard work and grabbing the right opportunities. His job was secure, though the money wasn't great. He had a house. And children who went to school. The only mosquito caught in his teeth was his wife. He wondered what Hat Man would say if he'd lived to meet her. He smiled. Hyena queen. That's what he'd say. Steel jaws to devour and eat people alive. Bad temper to poison even the sweetest relationship.

Losing Hat Man had been the worst day of his life—more traumatic even than seeing his mother stretched out on the floor, dead. He never saw it coming. Hat Man picked the wrong victim. It is true that Hat Man cried if he ever discovered he'd taken food from a very hungry person. It is also true he never took more than the two of them needed. And it was a fact that his plans never included injury or pain. But it is a mystery why he chose the man in the suit.

The man's shiny new car bounced to a halt next to them on the dirt track that he and Hat Man strolled along. The man, wearing a dark green suit, rolled down his car window and rested his elbow on the window sill. "*Sanibonani*," he said with an unfamiliar accent.

"Do you know where Mrs. Bunduzi's house is?"

Hat Man peered through the man's window to the passenger seat. A leather briefcase lay open on it. A small laptop computer was tucked inside next to a cell phone. "We can show you," he said. But he knew Mrs. Bunduzi as well as he knew the President of South Africa: not at all. He led the man down to an isolated spot where a small bridge crossed a churning brown river, then ran round the back of the car to the passenger widow and tapped on the window. He pointed to the left rear tire. "You have a flat tire," he shouted.

When the man opened the door to inspect it, Hat Man snapped open the passenger door, grabbed the briefcase and ran. The two boys headed into brush and reeds growing along the river banks. But the man's legs were powered by strong wind. He caught Hat Man and flipped him onto the path. The boy's head bounced on a rock and before his eyes closed in death, he whispered, "I'm sorry *numzane*, sir."

That was a long time ago. But remembering still brought pain. For so long now he had trained himself to capture all the memories of the past, stuff them into the cupboard of his mind, and shut the door. But more and more the door was flying open and like catching a fog, he just couldn't return them to his safe place.

He'd trusted no one since that day. No one was his friend.

CHAPTER 26

It was here at last. Friday. A knot of anxiety twisted in Ida's stomach. It was now or never. If ever she needed help, it was today. Washing dishes at the sink, she could hear splashing and shouts from the Van Reenen's pool. Her neighbors were back. Sounded like someone was having fun.

She stepped over the window to see who it was through the gap in the hedge. The phone rang. She wiped her hands on a kitchen towel, switched off the oven, and ran for the phone, but it stopped ringing as she picked it up. She turned back to the kitchen when the phone rang again. She snatched it up. "Oh, hi, Shell. Did you just call?" She waited for the usual light-hearted nonsense to start but Shell sounded out of breath.

"I'm on the Nelspruit road." Ida waited for her to continue. "There are bodies strewn across the road. The…"

"Slow down, Shell. What's happened?

"There's been a horrible accident at the bottom of the hill… you know where the road takes a bend up to Riverside Mall? A double-long bus has overturned and it's blocking the four lanes of road. And there's a taxi-van lying on its side on the grass verge. Must have collided. Windows on the bus have blown out. Bodies everywhere." She gasped. Silence. Then, "The taxi. It's moving," this was so soft Ida could only just hear her. "There's someone still alive in it."

Ida could hear Shell breathing heavily. "That's awful, Shell" she said. "Are the police there yet?"

Shell said nothing. Finally she said, "Sorry Ida, I have to go. Oh, yes, the police came a minute or so ago and I can see two ambulances trying to skim past all the cars backing up the hill. It's five o'clock traffic. This place is going to be a zoo." She hung up.

Ida replaced the phone. What do you do or say when something like this happens? What's going to happen to all those children whose parents are not coming home tonight–ever? As it is, so many children have only one parent, if they're lucky. Who's going to feed them?

She disappeared into her bedroom and shut the door behind her and flung herself onto the bed. "Lord, what am I supposed to say to you? I don't know how to pray for all these families. It's all so big. Please, please help them. Send people to comfort them."

She heard the door opening and felt a tug at her arm. "*Mama*?" She heard footsteps round the bed then felt a curly head rest on the quilt next to her. She stared into two brown eyes. "Hello, Surprise." She tried to smile. His look of concern remained.

"I am sad," she said, not knowing how much to tell him. "A bus fell over and some people are hurt. I am talking to Jesus about it." An arm snaked around her shoulders. Ida drew him close and felt the sweet smell of the child. "Please keep this one safe, Lord." she said.

The phone rang in the living room. "I need to answer that." She squeezed Surprise and jumped off the bed. She snatched up the phone. "Hello."

"Mrs. Morgan? This is Sergeant Jawena."

"I was just going to call you, Sergeant. How are the plans for tonight?"

"That's what I am phoning about. I have a problem."

Ida held her breath. Please don't say you can't do it.

"There has been a very bad accident."

"The double-bus and the taxi?"

"I am there right now. It is very bad. There are many dead. It will take a long time to sort it all out. I do not think we can go to Masoyi tonight. We need all the staff we can get."

"But it may be our only opportunity to get the men."

"Mrs. Morgan, I am very sorry. I have children. They are the blood that beats in my body. I know how important this is for you. I promise we will do all we can to find these men. But we cannot do it today. I think it will be many hours before we leave here."

Ida replaced the phone, feeling the last ray of hope disappear into despair. "This is not fair! It must be done tonight. They're going to get away with it and do it to other children." She picked up a cushion and threw it at the window. "Lord, don't you care…?" What was she saying? "Sorry, Lord. I know it's not your fault and you do care, deeply."

She heard the shuffle of feet in the doorway. "Oh, boy." She settled herself and prepared to look happy.

Moses and Bandile stood inside the living room door. "*Mama*, Bandile say I must help him get a drink." How quickly life reverted to its natural rhythm.

"Bandile, show me your muscles. See, you're a big boy, you can

131

do it. Moses will help you if you need it."

Back to her problem. If the police couldn't help her get the men, was it possible for her to do something–with a little help, of course? Some of the men in the street might be willing to do something? Her mind began to scheme. How could they catch the men? Easing herself down into her favorite chair she began to work out a plan. The more she thought about it, the more she realized how it depended on so many 'ifs.' *If* she could persuade her neighbors to help her. *If* the abusers actually appeared tonight. *If* they could entice them into the house. If. If. *If.*

But the more she thought about it, the more excited she became. A simple plan began to form. It could work. She would never forgive herself for not trying. She hurried over to her desk and scribbled a list of all the things she would need. Her first priority was recruiting able-bodied helpers. After a few instructions to Moses, she let herself out the back door.

First she had to go to the Van Reenens next door. She couldn't have done this a week ago. Funny how much bolder you become when you know a person's weaknesses. The power they have over you evaporates and leaves you with the strength of reality. She rang the gate bell. No one answered. She rang again. Still no response. Some of her newfound bravado began to slip. Was she making a mistake? She tried one more time.

"Yes?" A tinny voice came through the intercom.

"Hello, Rene. It's Ida from next door. Is Japie there?"

"Hang on, Ida." The gate began to grumble open. "Come in."

Rene appeared at the front door. A mop of curls appeared at her elbow.

"Estelle! *Jy lyk so goed.* You look so good." The child smiled up at Ida. "How are you?" Ida bent down to her level.

The child pointed to the band-aid on her leg. "A snake bit me on the leg."

"*Wie's dit?*" Japie's voice came from behind Rene. "Who is it?" His head appeared over his wife's shoulder. "Oh. It's you, Ida."

Ida straightened. Obviously Japie hadn't attended any 'Love your Enemy' classes recently... ever. She stepped back down a couple of steps to look up at him. "Japie, I need your help."

He leaned against the door frame and picked at his well-shaped fingernails. He said nothing, so she took that as a 'go ahead.'

Once more she found herself saying, "It's a long story." While she explained briefly, Japie continued to study his nails. She stopped what she was saying in mid-sentence and glared at him. He suddenly realized she wasn't speaking and his head shot up.

"I'm listening," he said.

She finished by telling him about the accident and the police's inability to help her tonight. "I'm hoping a few men in the street will join us. If we go as a group, I know we can catch these men. We only have a small window of opportunity and it is tonight."

Japie glared at her. "Let the police handle it some other time. It's their business."

Rene nudged him in the ribs but he kept staring at Ida. "Stay out of this, Rene."

This was going to be harder than Ida anticipated. "Japie, you are a loving father. If someone hurt Estelle you'd do everything in your power to find the people who hurt her and bring them to justice, wouldn't you?"

Japie's neck and cheeks grew red but he said, "Well, they're not my kids. Let their own people help them."

"Japie." Rene spoke through clenched teeth.

"Rene, take Estelle inside." His eyes remained on Ida. "Now!"

Ida had a sudden urge to help him feel pain. Instead, she decided to help him get in touch with his dark side.

"Japie, I understand your gardener, Samson, saved Estelle's life."

For the first time uncertainty entered his fierce expression.

"Maybe." Still defiant.

"Talk on the street is that he had to take himself to hospital afterwards. What happened?"

For the first time, Ida almost felt pity for the man. His expression exposed it all. A naked display of guilt and shame. He blustered on, making excuses and justifying himself. Ida listened without interjecting. Finally she said, "Japie, nobody's children become everybody's children, for good or bad. I choose for good. I'm going to talk to some of the other men on the street. If you change your mind, call me."

She turned away and made her way to the Nkosi family next door. Stanley was easing his red Toyota Corolla through the gate and into his garage. While she waited for him to clamber out of the car, the front door opened and his three children rushed out.

"*Baba*," they shouted, clinging onto his legs and arms and pulling him to the house.

He looked apologetically at Ida and spoke to his children. "*Yima*. Stop. Let me talk to Mrs. Morgan. I am coming now." The children let him go and scampered back into the house.

"Mr. Nkosi," she corrected herself, "Stanley, I need your help. Again." For the next few minutes Ida explained her idea to catch the men. Stanley interrupted her only when he needed clarification. When he agreed to help her, she shouted, "Yes!"

"We need to be able to defend ourselves so bring whatever you have that's legal. They talked about what kind of weapons or defensive gear they should take and Stanley said he'd bring something.

Ida had an idea. "Stanley, do you have an iPhone or something similar?"

"I do."

"Would you bring it? I need you to do something when we have the men in custody. Tell you when things are finalized."

One down, three to go. If she could get three more men they could do it. She concluded by saying, "I'll pick you up at six o'clock."

She hurried out the gate and headed for the Bothas. By 5:45, Koos Botha and Piet Willemse were also on board. Without Japie's help Ida would have to rearrange the plan but it might still work.

"I'll take my Jeep as well so we can get right down to the children's houses. You never know what could happen out there," Koos said. "Someone could get hurt and have to be taken out quickly. Better to be safe than sorry." Good thinking.

"I think we should dress in dark clothes," Piet said. "There won't be electric lights but the full moon will make us very vulnerable."

That done, there was only about 45 minutes of daylight left. They needed to go. Ida got together her 'just in case' list of things and threw them into the boot of the car. Camera, binoculars, rope, torch, strong tape, firewood, newspaper, matches. She needed to check that Pete had remembered to bring a large cardboard box and Stanley, his phone. As she slammed down the boot lid she heard her phone ringing. Should she get it? There wasn't much time. Maybe, just maybe, it was Sergeant Jawena saying he could come after all. She dashed inside and snatched up the phone.

"Ida, it's Rene. What did you say to Japie? He says he's going with you. He says he can't let a woman go into a dangerous situation without some protection. He told me to tell you..." she hesitated. "Sorry, Ida, but he says he will not take orders from a woman so... ah... he..."

"Rene, please tell him this is not about gender nor who's in charge. It's about protecting children. I have a plan and it will work if we stick to it. If he doesn't want to come, that's up to him."

"One more thing," Rene continued, "my car is still in the garage and I need to go to a meeting tonight. If Japie still wants to come, is it okay if he goes with you?"

"No problem. I'll stop by your house in case he decides to come. Be there in about five minutes." She put down the phone and shook her head. They needed him but she wasn't begging.

He was there. Leaning against his brick gateway.

It was a strange journey. Ida led the way. She had picked up Stanley first and he sat in the front with her. Next came Japie who, when he saw Stanley sitting next to Ida, looked as though he was about to scuttle back inside. "Jump in, Japie." Ida said. "Better sit behind me. There'll be more room for your legs. The big man folded himself inside and sat with his head poking between his knees.

"Just got to stop at Shelly's." Ida eased the car off the road onto Shelly's driveway, tooted the horn, then ran to the gate and waited. Shelly came running out holding a cell phone which she passed through the bars to Ida. "You're the best, Shelly. I'll bring it back tomorrow." I hope.

"Be careful," Shelly shouted after her.

Walking back to her car, Ida saw Koos was parked behind her, his Jeep idling. They set off. Ida checked every now and then that Koos' car was still following her.

Japie said nothing for the first ten minutes. Finally he said, "I brought my gun."

"Japie, we don't want any violence." Ida felt like his mother.

"There is no way I am going to put myself in danger without being able to defend myself."

"If you do something stupid or rash, I'm not going to cover for you."

"I never do anything stupid or rash."

Ja, right.

She went over her plan in her head. She threw out an 'olive branch' to Japie. "Once we've got them, would you guard the door, Japie? We need someone who will convince them we're serious. You're the right guy." Japie grunted from behind her. At least he wasn't fighting her on this one.

As they turned off the main road onto the track, Ida noticed the chicken man had gone home but his empty chicken hutch was still there.

Driving up the rutted road, Ida was thankful the sun had disappeared over the ridge of the hill and wasn't shining directly into her eyes. Japie had stopped talking. She snatched a glance in her mirror. Interesting. His face was calm... like a man about to walk into his destiny.

At the crest of the hill, Ida passed the cemetery and came to a stop before the car became visible from below. "Let's meet with the other guys and go over the plan." She jumped out and hurried over to Koos and Piet as they pulled up behind her car. She heard the car door slam behind her, and Japie and Stanley appeared next to her.

"Okay," she started, "the children live just down the hill there. I first want to check to see that there's no one there. Then we can go down. Koos, you'll notice a burnt-out farm house about halfway down, then a group of three houses at the bottom of the hill. I'm going to park behind the farm house. You can travel right down to the houses. There are some large bushes at the rear of the furthest house–big enough to hide the car." The men nodded as she disclosed the plan in more detail.

From out the boot of her car she pulled out her binoculars. Careful not to be too conspicuous she scanned the area around the children's houses. "There's no sign of life yet," she called to the men. "Japie, why don't you and Stanley go down with Koos? I'll join you as soon as I'm ready." She poked her head through Koos's window and spoke to him. "When you get there would you start building the fire in the pit straight away? Make it quite big. We could be waiting a while." She handed over a plastic packet containing firewood. "Piet, would you set up your box in the furthest corner of the house–in the room adjoining the first room."

They set off slowly, bumping down the hill. She followed, praying fervently that everything would go according to plan. As she drew near the farmhouse, she veered right, following what could have been the original farm road. Behind that pile of weed-covered bricks looked like a good place to conceal the car. She pulled in as far as she could and then jumped out to see if it was visible from the road. It wasn't.

Moses had told her the man always left his car between the first two trees in a row of trees lining the farmhouse garden. Those massive gum trees must be the ones Moses meant. She walked through the knee-high grass to where Moses had indicated, willing herself not to think of snakes.

Sure enough, between the first and second trees, she came across a small patch of ground which looked as though it could have been used for parking. Some of the grass had flattened along two wide though distinct lines. Shaped and pressed down by car tires, she guessed. Certainly, it was the most obvious place to park a car. Bending over, she began her search. Over that small area, the litter was more prevalent. Someone had spent time here.

Using a pair of kitchen tongs she carefully picked up a couple of cigarette butts, a coke can and two different chip packets and slipped them into an unused Ziploc bag. This wouldn't be admissible in court but it might initiate a closer search of the area for forensic evidence.

She placed the bag carefully in her boot and then took out a plastic bag,

Shell's cell phone, a camera, cushion and a small glass jar. She walked back to the man's 'parking place,' unscrewing the jar as she went. She emptied the contents in a line between the trees. Now it was time to join the men.

Nice. From where she walked, the jeep was not visible. Entering the last house, she saw the large box had been assembled and placed upside-down in a corner of Moses' house. The window closest to it was open wide. One last check on Shell's cell phone. Volume of ring–LOUD. Battery–full. She bent down, placed the phone carefully on the inside of the box, and taped it on the bottom. On the inside flaps of the box, she placed two bricks to hold it down and to give an initial impression of someone inside holding it down.

Off to Samson and Phineas's house. From out of the plastic bag, she pulled scraps of leftover food and placed them on a tin plate. This she left next to the boys' blanket. Next she grabbed the old broom that sat against the doorway. It was probably one their mother had made by tying strands of elephant grass to a stick with twine. Somewhat concerned that its severely depleted bristles wouldn't sweep properly, Ida intensified her efforts, but was satisfied when it did a passable job—enough to give it that lived in feeling, anyway.

She left the door open a little and proceeded to Promise's house where she duplicated her efforts. Lastly, she spruced up the fire area, sweeping it clean and placed a pot next to the fire to which Piet was putting the finishing touch. The men needed to think the children were still living here. If this plan wasn't going to work, it wouldn't be because she missed some small detail.

The short African twilight was almost done when Ida called the men together.

Koos walked up with his contribution to the defense effort: a hefty, mahogany walking stick.

"What you got there, Grandpa?" Stanley asked him.

Koos shook it in his face. "At least it's not an ornamental stabbing spear that's held together with office glue." He grinned. He grabbed hold of the tip of the spear in Stanley's hand. "Hey, it's sticky. What did you do to it?" He snatched his fingers away.

"Just sharpened it and dipped it in poison."

Koos' color paled to a bleached grey. "You're teasing, right?"

Stanley shrugged. "Maybe. Maybe not." He saw the look in Koos' eyes. "Only works on the bad guys."

Koos punched him on the arm.

Stanley slapped his thigh and bared his white teeth in a huge grin. "Got you."

"Hey, Piet, what you got tucked in your belt?" Japie spoke up, looking as though he'd woken up from a long sleep.

Piet looked defensive.

"A gun?" Japie's mouth open. "I thought you said you didn't own one?"

"I don't. It's my son's."

"Your son is six years old," Koos said.

"It's a squirt gun." That was it. The other men looked at each other and howled. Japie threw back his head and guffawed. So he was human.

The corner of Piet's mouth slid up. "It looks real. You never know, it may come in use."

While Ida watched the men slap and kid each other that same warmth she'd been experiencing recently flowed over her. But, time to move.

"Did you bring anything a little more… age-appropriate?" Ida said when the laughter lessened.

Piet reached behind his bag on the ground bringing out a short handled machete. "I sharpened it just in case." After grunts of approval they were back on track.

Before Ida could say anything, Japie spoke up, "One more thing." He eased a hand into his back pocket and brought a small, round flat tin and a piece of rag. "It's going to be bright out tonight with the full moon. Black shoe polish will give us a bit more camouflage."

He dipped a rag into the tin and in seconds all that stood out on him was the whites of his eyes." He handed the tin to Koos.

Stanley grabbed the tin from Koos. "I need a touch up." He patted his black face.

The men erupted. The muscles around Japie's mouth quivered but he remained in control. "Stop fooling around." He stepped over to Ida. "You must go and wait in the car or bushes or somewhere." Japie said. "We can handle it from here."

"Okay, Japie." She glanced around the circle. "Any questions before I go?" No questions. "We're going to catch these guys." Ida tucked the cushion under her arm and disappeared behind a bush closest to the path. Hopefully there'd be reason to thank them properly later.

CHAPTER 27

As the curtain of darkness fell, the moon rose silently behind Ida, a massive red orb emerging from the horizon. She turned around to watch it as it gradually turned white and lit the world with its soft, clear light.

From where Ida sat on her cushion, moving aside a larger branch in front of her allowed her to see the area quite well. She faced the hill down which the men would arrive. Behind the furthest wall of Moses' house, and to her left, hid Piet and Stanley. Koos and Japie waited behind the second house.

Any other time she would be reveling in the fresh beauty of the night. A comforting murmur of conversation reached her. She snatched a moment to close her eyes, raise her face to the sky, and feel the flutter of cool breeze against her skin.

The minutes passed. Ida stretched her legs in front of her and straightened her neck. She raised her watch to catch the light of the moon. Time slowed down. Her mind began to wander as she settled down to wait.

Patience was not her Tony's strong point. When he grew tired of waiting, his toes began to wriggle. The longer he waited, the more frantic the movement. If he wore shoes, you could see the knuckle bumps rise and fall as his toes fought for room to move. The tops of his shoes were always the first to wear down. But when he was with her, his toes never moved.

Except for the time when they were first married. She'd locked the keys in their only car. He came running out of the house, his briefcase in hand. "I'm late for my meeting with Henry."

"I locked the keys in the car."

"Well, go and get the spare."

"They're in my handbag."

He sucked in his breath. "Get your handbag then…Sweetheart."

"It's in the car." That's when she looked down and noticed his shoes.

"Did you know your shoes are dancing?"

He stared down at his shoes for several seconds, speechless. Then, "Ida! Open the door."

She ran.

She couldn't remember any more how they opened the car door

but from that day his impatience became known as the Dance of the Knuckle Bumps. For some reason, whenever she drew attention to his shoes, the greater the commotion inside them became. She smiled at the thought.

She was thinking happy thoughts and it felt good. But she needed to concentrate. When she looked again, the moon had moved to just behind her shoulder. Thirty minutes. She looked again. Fifty minutes. An hour. The longer the wait, the greater the gap for doubt. Had she made a bad mistake? Would the guys forgive her for wasting their evening?

"Look at the time." Japie's voice carried clearly to her, breaking into her mental doodling. "I'm giving it five more minutes then I'm gone."

You can't give in now. Please, please, please. Just a little longer.

Then she heard it. The faint drone of a car. She whistled and got an answering reply followed by silence. She kept her eyes on the dark outline of the top of the hill. A pair of headlights appeared and for a brief moment seemed suspended in space then dropped down as the car began to descend. As the car drew nearer she could make out the unmistakable sound of a VW engine.

Was that what Moses was trying to tell her? Ida became aware of her thumping heart and her throat constricting. What if her plan didn't work? What if people got hurt? A bit late for that. She brought her attention back to the car lights bobbing over the rough surface of the track.

Finally the car rolled to a stop between the first two gum trees to the left of her, above the houses—just as Moses said it would. A car door flung open and loud voices were carried down to her. Three men extricated themselves from the small car, jostling and ribbing each other. Then, as clear as though he were standing next to her, she heard a man say, "Here's a torch. Remember, sometimes they hide in the last house. That is good. It will be easy for you. But look first in the other houses." A pause. "Don't forget they will run away if they know you are there."

Slurred voices and stumbling along the path told a story. How much difference did it make that the men were drinking? Ida wasn't sure if it was a good thing or not. Their reflexes may be dulled, but were her group of rescuers equipped to handle men who were

141

belligerent and unpredictable?

Incoming porcupine. This was no longer just a plan. The men were here. There was no telling what they would do if they saw Ida or her group. Hiding behind the bush, Ida knew now was a good time to tell herself the truth. The men didn't know she was there and didn't appear to be expecting anyone. She was safe for the moment. Hardly allowing herself to blink, she watched them come. Closer. One. Two of them passed by. The last man drew parallel to her bush.

"I am coming." He stopped and faced her from the outside of the bush while the other men lurched on. Ida felt her heart go into overdrive. Her breathing grew shallow. Did he know she was there? Wafts of fetid breath reached her through the maze of twigs and branches and made her want to hurl. She could hear him fuss with his clothing, but couldn't tell what he was doing because he was to her a mere shadow. Then she felt a stream of warm liquid hit her sandaled feet. Heard it smack the dust around her. She grabbed her mouth and squeezed her lips tightly together. If she screamed now they were in big trouble.

The man pulled up his zipper and followed the others. The urge to run away was overwhelming, but into her mind came nine little black faces and with them the resolve to finish what she had started.

She pulled her thoughts back to what was happening with the others. The first two men barged into the first house. Ida glimpsed flashes of light as they searched for any children there. On to the next house.

"Wait for me."

Ida recognized the voice as the man who sprayed her. When his footsteps disappeared around the house, she rose silently from her position and slipped over to the side of the first house.

"There is no one in the first house." A man said in a stage whisper. Then it came. Ida heard the faint sound of children's laughter coming from Shell's cell in the large box. Good job, Piet.

The men stopped suddenly and listened. Whispering just loud enough for Ida to hear, one said, "They are in the last house." The voice was barely audible. Ida couldn't make out the whispers that followed, but she sidled up to the edge of the house, hoping the squelching in her sandals wasn't as loud as it appeared to her. She hunched down and peered around the corner. Two of the men stood close together at the door while the third one wandered over to the almost extinct fire, a bottle to his lips. He lowered himself onto the concrete slab that made up the fire pit. She suddenly realized that the men were all dressed in business suits.

"I must finish my drink," the last man said, loud enough to alert anyone halfway back to White River.

"Shhh." The other two beckoned for him to come.

He raised a shaky hand. "They are not going anywhere. I will come when I'm ready. Keep the youngest one for me."

Anger poured into Ida's soul. She felt its heat in her face. She shook her head. Shelve it, Ida. Back to the men. The only way the plan could work was if they were all together in one house. Ida swung back against the wall her head tilted upward. "Help, Lord."

"We are tired of waiting. Come *now*." A whisper from a man at the door, "We go in." The man nearest the door reached out a hand and slowly pulled down the handle. He switched on his torch and stepped quietly into the room. The second man turned quickly and motioned the man at the fire to come inside.

"Come," he said, then moved into the house. Noise erupted inside–what sounded to Ida like a wrecking crew. Sounds of household items being hurled against the walls, along with swearing and shouting.

Somehow in the din, the cell phone rang out its laughter for a couple of seconds. "They're in the box." She briefly heard the sound of running feet. Ida kept her eyes on the man on the ground. His head was up. Listening; but he was in no hurry.

For goodness sake, get inside.

Ida held her breath and prayed. The man outside drained the last of the beer, raised the bottle above his upturned face, and allowed the last few drops of liquid to drip onto the tip of his tongue. He threw the bottle onto the sand and loudly relieved himself of a build up of gas. He leaned forward to rise when a series of low grunts, vaguely like a giant frog, emanated from behind the third house. The man became instantly alert.

Warthog?

The man spun around as he searched for the animal in the shadows. The second set of grunts sent the man flying into the house to join the others and slam the door behind him. From around the corner, the dark figure of Japie appeared and slipped silently next to the closed door of the house. He readied the weapon in his right hand and the torch in his left just as a yell came from the bedroom.

"It's a trick. The children are not here."

Japie snatched open the door and aimed a piercing beam of light into the house together with his gun. At that moment Ida could forgive Japie anything.

"You are surrounded." His voice thundered through the night. "There are men waiting for you at the windows so don't try to get out there."

Up the hill the VW's engine roared into life.

"There's someone still in the car," Koos yelled from the far side of the house.

"He won't be going very far." Ida shouted back and ran up to Japie. She took a quick look up the hill. The car bumbled and bounced backward 50 paces or so, then stopped. The interior light came on as the door opened and a figure bailed out the door.

That bottle of assorted nails thrown across the path had done their work.

There was the flash of a man running in front of the car, silhouetted against the headlights. He fled up the hill into the night. Even if the man got away, the car should hold enough evidence to identify him. Ida turned back to Japie.

"Koos, phone the police," Japie shouted without taking his eyes off the closed door. "They must be finished processing the accident by now."

"Ask for Sergeant Jawena," Ida said in his ear. "He's the one I've been dealing with." While Koos phoned the police, Ida returned to her hideout behind the bush. Scooping up her camera she made her way to the window side of the house where Piet and Stanley stood guard, weapons raised.

She found a position slightly behind Stanley, who faced the window. His eyes watched the men, his spear rested on his shoulder, ready to strike. Ida whispered, "Hey, Stanley, you make a great warthog."

"It wasn't me."

"Me either." Koos stood opposite the first window his walking stick at the ready.

"You mean there really is a wild animal out here?"

When she saw the gleam of Stanley's teeth she turned to Koos. The same.

"You rats," she rolled her eyes. "But you were good." She peered through the grimy window. On the cupboard, the men's torch flickered feebly. It wouldn't last much longer. The men sat in a close circle facing each other and whispering.

She crept over to Stanley. "Now's a good time to put your phone on the window sill. Let's see if we can record anything incriminating."

She tried to hear what they said. Could they keep them here until the police arrived? She strained to see the face of her watch. If the police came immediately, they should be here in about 30 minutes—that would make it 10:30. Any time sooner would suit her very well.

The man who had sprayed her sat on the couch nearest the window. She pressed back against the wall; there in the shadows, Ida watched him. It was like observing the build up of a major storm. While she strained to hear the conversation, a picture began to emerge as she pieced together phases and key words. What she didn't hear of the man's words he showed clearly with his body.

"You said there was no risk...respectable business... connections in Mpumalanga... If anything happens to me...watch..." He jumped up, searching for something in the room. When the other men saw him they were up and ready to defend themselves.

One of the men held up his hands and said slowly and deliberately, "The man who told us was...ser..."

Ida leaned forward to hear but the words fell short of her ears.

"I don't care who he is." His voice exploded. "He could be the Chief of Police for all I care but if we go to jail, you will..."

Did she hear right? There was no time to think more about it. The angry man took hold of the man nearest him and grabbed him by the neck. Ida took the opportunity. Good time for the camera. Widen the window. She curled her fingers round the window knob to unscrew it; with her other hand she held the camera. Almost open, the window knob resisted, squealing on rusty hinges.

As one, all three men swung her way. The angry man cried out and lunged at her. She took aim through the opening and squeezed the camera button. A white flash. Inside, the man's body rammed against the windowsill with a forceful thump just as she stumbled back. His arm shot through the window, fingers scrabbling for her. Koos heaved his walking stick down. It struck the windowsill next to the man's arm, radiating a mighty boom through the night. The man's arm disappeared in an instant, his eyes wide and staring as he backed away.

"Stanley, what's happening?" Japie shouted from the far side of the house.

"It is okay," Stanley yelled back.

Ida whispered in Stanley's ear, "Have we got enough to hang them in court yet?"

Not waiting for the answer, Ida ran around the house to let Japie know what had happened. "Japie, I'm going to see if there's anything in the car that will tell us who the driver is."

Truthfully? Sitting around and waiting was way too stressful.

"Be careful. Don't touch anything."

Ida nodded, picked up her torch and in a gentle lope, made her way up the hill. Part-way up the hill, the lights of the car lit up the path, making it easier for her to see. The car battery would eventually run down with the lights on. Why should she care? She switched them off anyway and then switched on the interior light.

That's when she saw it. Her gaze moved up to the window. There it was: the nasty crack in the windscreen. She went cold. It was the man from the other day. He must have been coming here. She shivered and pulled herself out the car. She slammed the door and leaned against the side of the car. At that moment she heard, for the second time that night, the sound of a vehicle arriving at the top of the hill.

Thank goodness. The police. She stopped to watch. *Wait.* That couldn't be the police. It was too soon. She had to tell the others. She locked the car and fled silently down the hill.

Japie stood as she had left him: his eyes fixed on the door, which was now closed, hands stretched taut before him.

"It's about time," he said.

"Japie, I don't think it's the police. It's only been fifteen minutes since we called them. There's a second group of men coming."

"Blast!"

"There's no way we can take them all."

"What do you suggest then?"

"Frighten them away?"

"That's stupid." Japie said.

"You have a better idea? Piet, what did the police say?"

"They're coming right now. I told them it was urgent."

"Okay, we have two problems. The police won't be here in time to help with the second batch of men. If the men in the house start making a noise, it may scare them off. That could be a good thing but it is too risky. The new guys could come and investigate, then we could lose all the men and end up in a free-for-all. Someone could get seriously hurt." The odds were bad. There were too few of them to do anything properly.

Maybe not. Ida spoke into Japie's ear. "What if we catch them all?"

"You're mad." Japie said.

"Maybe, but trying has a hundred percent more potential than not trying." There was no time to explain her plan. "Japie, I need you to trust me. Switch off your light. Keep your gun on the door but stay in the shadows." She turned to Piet. "Get out your son's gun and machete and hide between the second and third houses. I'm going to lure them into the second house. Be ready to guard the door of the second house."

She dashed around to Nkosi and Koos. "More men are coming. We're going to catch them in the second house. Koos, the moon is casting shadows on this side of the house. Be ready with your stick at the window but stand back in the shadows." Over to Nkosi. "Do you play the drums?"

"Not really."

"Good. Go into the second house with your spear. In the first room, under a sheet, is a big drum. Put it in a corner where it is darkest, where the men cannot see you from the window. When Koos gives you the signal, start playing the drum. Thump your feet and hum in a high-pitched voice like a child. I don't know–whatever you do when you play a drum." Back to Koos. "When I shake the bush I'm hiding behind it's the signal for Nkosi to start drumming. Tell him straight away. When the men reach the house, I will run to the window and let you know when to stop playing. Stop immediately. Grab your spear and stand behind the door. As soon as the men are inside, guard them from the doorway."

No more time. Ida raced to her original position behind the bush and hid. She felt fairly confident the drum would disguise any sound the men in the other house made and at the same time entice the men into the correct house.

Within seconds the area was still. The breeze gave no inkling of all that had happened so far that evening. Even the men were quiet. The scare the angry man had received at the window appeared to have subdued him into silence.

Halfway down the hill, the car stopped directly behind the stationary car, lighting the VW with the beam of its headlights. Only two people climbed out. Thank goodness. A man's words, at first soft but distinct, floated over to her. "We should come back another time. Someone is already here."

"No. See the tire it is flat." The other man must have tried the VW's door. "It is locked."

"Come on. Let us have some fun." The men set down the hill at a brisk pace heading directly toward Ida. Leading the way was a short, insubstantial man, with a dark cap pulled down low on his face. He chatted to the man behind him, his voice carrying clearly through the fresh night. As he drew closer, Ida could see him silhouetted against the night sky. She noticed something distinctive about his gait. It bothered her. He walked–no, he bounced on skinny legs as though his knees were strung with bungee cord. She'd seen this man before. Where? When? She searched the memory files of her mind. Where had she seen him?

They disappeared from view as the path took them round a bend. She could hear their feet crunching through a patch of debris. Very close now.

She checked Nkosi and Koos. Neither was visible. When she turned back, the men had stopped.

"Okay," the first man said, "we must not frighten them away. Go quietly."

That voice. She knew that voice too. She sucked in her breath. Then it hit her. It was the man who had killed Tony.

CHAPTER 28

How could she ever forget that voice? And those legs? The last time she'd seen them they'd been charging down her garden path toward Tony. The man was screaming, "Stop! I will shoot!" His gun jerked around in his hand. "Stop! You come any more I will kill you."

Tony put up his hands. "It's okay. I just want to talk to y…"

The man slapped his free hand to the gun-hand to steady the trembling and raised it to eye level. A second man rushed up to the gunman. He reached out a hand to steady his friend, saying, "Be careful!" But the action triggered something in the gunman's overwrought mind. A shot exploded in the night. Tony crumpled to the ground. By the time it was all over, Tony was no longer breathing.

He only wanted to talk to you. Murderer!

Ida thought she would collapse. These past two years she'd visualized every detail of what she would do to the man who killed her Tony if she ever had the chance. Now he stood before her and she was a stranded jellyfish.

From the faint rustle of leaves Ida knew they must be close by. They came abreast of where she was. She grabbed hold of the lower branches of the bush and rattled it. The men stopped. Listened.

"Shhh." Silence.

"There's something in the bush."

The second man grabbed the arm of the small man and stared down at him. "Maybe we come another time?"

"What is the matter? You are a girl?"

Inside the drumming began. Hesitantly at first. Humming. The men stopped arguing and crept towards the house to listen. The killer pointed to the second house and edged up to the window. He peered inside. He put his hand up to his face to shield his eyes from the reflection of moonlight on the window.

He shrugged and pulled his friend by the arm. The two of them disappeared around the house. Ida sped to the window. "Nkosi, they're coming." She dropped out of sight. The drumming stopped.

A few seconds later the door creaked open. Wider. Whispering. A yell. "Stop. Right where you are!" Raised voices. Ida could hear Nkosi directing the men. Then, once more she sprinted up the hill to the men's Citi Golf. No one was going anywhere in this car either. Not tonight. She bent down and unscrewed the air-cap in the left front tire. When she heard the soft stream of escaping air she moved to the back tire and did the same.

She lent against the car and waited. Not for long. For the third time that night, she heard the drone of a vehicle. Then car lights materialized at the top of the hill. The police? She had to make sure. A second car emerged. Blue lights glowed above both windscreens. Thank goodness. She ran around to the driver side of the Golf, snatched open the door, and hit the emergency flasher button. The first police van veered toward the blinking lights and rolled to a stop just behind the Golf. Sergeant Jawena lumbered out. There was no customary greeting. He stared beyond the car she was standing next to, to the VW Beetle. "Is Officer Dube already here? He called in sick this morning."

But it was Ida who felt sick. "He's come and gone."

Jawena frowned. "I did not know you called him." Ida could tell he was piqued that an underling had been informed before he was.

"Officer Dube *brought* the men we caught tonight. He was waiting for them in his car but ran away when he heard us seize them."

"Mrs. Morgan, he… What?" A look of deep confusion crossed his face. "You mean…"

"He has been making a little profit on the side."

Jawena hung his shaking head. Then he straightened his shoulders. "Tell me quickly what happened. Then you better take us down there."

Ida briefly filled him in, including the fact her husband's killer was amongst them.

"Mrs. Morgan, how do you know they came for the children?"

"I believe I can prove it to you. Sergeant, there's just one thing I still need to do though. Give me five minutes. Please?"

"I'm listening."

"When you surround the house, stand next to the window so you can hear what's being said. We have a cell phone recording the men's conversations but I don't trust the battery to last long enough. We need you to hear what the men say. But if the men know you're there, they won't talk."

He agreed. "I'll give you exactly five minutes then I'm going in. Be careful. When you are done, find a safe place away from the houses." She slipped silently down the hill. This better work.

"Stanley," she whispered behind him. "The police are here but there's something I'd like you to do first." A quick explanation and he waited for Jawena's men to move into position. The Sergeant appeared beside him and signaled him to begin. Stanley moved closer to the window and spoke to the men inside.

"*Sanibonani.*" His voice was respectful. "May I ask you a question?" He had their attention. He checked the area around him then leaned conspiratorially forward, dropping his voice. "Why did you let Officer Dube, a policeman, bring you here? You know he will testify against you and send you to prison?"

The angry man rose and took a step toward the window. "What do you mean? He contacted us."

"Maybe it was a trap to get you here."

"Rubbish, Officer Dube brought that man here before." The angry man pointed to a man sitting at the edge of the sofa, his face in his hands. "When the children were living here. Afterwards, that man paid Officer Dube and the policeman took him home."

"I have heard enough." Jawena disappeared around the house to the door where Japie still stood guard. "This is the police!" Instant quiet in the two houses. "Come out with your hands above your heads."

No one moved. Jawena's voice rose. "If we have to come in to you, we cannot guarantee your safety." Two officers hammered on each door of the two houses.

One by one, the men stumbled into the clearing, their hands behind their heads. Last outside, the angry business man strode through the door.

"Mr. Kuanda." Jawena stared at him. "It is indeed a night of surprises. What are you doing here?"

"I was brought here under false pretences." He folded his arms then unfolded them to straighten his belt and adjust his collar, all the time looking away from the sergeant.

"What were you expecting? Police protection?" Jawena gripped the man's coat sleeve and propelled him toward the group who were being lined up in pairs and handcuffed to each other. Officers trained guns at them and then marched them to the police vans.

As Tony's killer approached Ida, she stepped into open. "Remember me?"

The man stumbled backward.

"You came to my house."

Puzzled. A shrug.

"I did not invite you or your gun."

The man's eye's widened.

"Did you think you had got away with murdering my husband?"

His face told the story. He knew. The policeman nearest him thrust a gun in his side. The man dropped his head and the procession shuffled on. Ida stared after them, the pounding in her chest now reached her ears. She began to tremble. She felt someone step next to her. It was Nkosi.

"Are you alright?"

She nodded. "Thank you. Thank you for everything." She lay a hand on his shoulder. "I'm sorry but you'll have to give the Sergeant your cell phone for evidence." She retrieved Shell's cell phone from the box, gathered up her belongings and started for her car. As she drew abreast of the umbrella thorn, she remembered. Turning round she hurried into the second house. She came out with a large drum tucked under her arm. After taking her load to her car she returned five minutes later and headed for a familiar bush, dropped onto hands and knees and disappeared into its thick foliage. Thirty seconds later she reversed out clutching a fist full of golf clubs, a ball of string and a wad of hessian.

"Now I'm done."

Once in the car, she stopped to look at her neighbors sitting with her in the shadows. "I couldn't have done this without you. I owe you. Big time. Thank you." The smiles told her all she wanted to know.

The two men replayed and rehashed the events of the night until Ida switched off and retreated into her own thoughts. She felt good about the outcome of the evening but an uncomfortable thought gnawed at her. It would never be totally over while Dube roamed free.

CHAPTER 29

For the second time in his life, Officer Dube was on the run. The ache in his chest, fed by the fear in his heart and the challenge of a steep hill, revealed the extent of his soft lifestyle. For a moment, he allowed himself a quick glimpse down the hill, but the mad drumming of blood in his ears blotted out any sounds. He tried to slow down his breathing so he could listen better. How had the police found out? He'd never shared his secret with anyone. Only the men he recruited knew and they wouldn't be foolish enough to talk.

All was quiet down there. What was going on? He strained to see through the darkness. No movement that he could see, just a faint flickering light in the window of the third house.

What if he told Sergeant Jawena his car had been stolen? "Did you find my car?" he could ask. But could he trust the men down there to keep quiet? He didn't even wait for the answer. That was ridiculous.

He must keep going. His life was slipping away and he couldn't stop it. It was all over. All the years of sacrifice to get where he was in the police force. All the promises he'd made to himself. He felt like an orphan again. He had to get away from here.

His first challenge was getting past the graveyard. He slowed down as the ground flattened and he could smell the mounds and rounds of new earth. His choice was either to find another way around the cemetery and possibly get lost, or go through it and risk the wrath of the Sitoko who hovered over the graves with malicious intent.

Fear of Man and the need for haste swung the balance in favor of the cemetery. He began to sing loudly to keep the Sitoko at bay. Prickles of apprehension crept up his spine as he advanced, step by careful step, through the graves. He kept his eyes focused ahead of him and tried not to think of his car and the protection and speed it could give him. Instead, stories of people who had angered the Sitoko flashed through his mind. Terrible stories of hearts ripped out and… He realized he'd stopped singing. Focus. Once he was through here—if he got through—he must find shelter for the night.

Almost there. One more grave.

Then he took off; his feet flew under him like a cheetah. Down the track, toward the safety of the main road. As he slowed down, so did the adrenalin shooting through his veins. His mind cleared and wandered back in time to his first run from home. It was a run fueled by fear just like this one, but at that time, others were responsible for creating the background to his history. Today he had created it.

The church couldn't help him this time. He'd squandered his opportunity to make something of his life.

He must move at night. It didn't matter where he was headed. Mozambique, though, was probably the nearest and safest place to hide. The shortest way to the coastal country was through the Kruger National Game Park. But how to avoid the wild animals? As a policeman, he knew how many illegal immigrants entering through the park ended up as lion food. Maybe if he could team up with some poachers? It was risky but at least they had guns. Where would he find them?

He shook his head. No, even he had his standards. Poachers were worse than the animals they slaughtered and as unpredictable as an angry hippo. He had to go round the long way.

He spent the next few hours scheming of ways to find food which wouldn't attract the attention of the police. He'd done it before. He could do it again.

He strode off along the main road. The lack of streetlights provided great cover for him. Every time a vehicle approached he changed his gait to look like an old man. Gradually, the number of cars decreased until he was alone on the road.

He made good time. As he reached the Plaston turn off, several police cars drove up behind him, plus a couple of civilian cars. They slowed down to look at him but he dropped his head and did the old man walk. They passed him and drove on.

He made good time. It was going to be okay. He felt an injection of energy and by dawn the next morning, he had walked through White River, and was well on his way to Nelspruit. As the sky lightened to pale blue, he noticed a path leading to a crop of rocks and large trees and chose a spot to hide for the day. If he was not mistaken, there was a small stream at the bottom of the hill. It was meant to be.

CHAPTER 30

There was great rejoicing the next day when Ida told the children about how the men had been arrested. She couldn't bring herself to tell them Dube had got away. All the children, except Moses, dispersed to play in the garden.

"*Mama*," she said, "you did not tell us how they got the man who brought the men in the car?"

Ida pulled herself up from her seat on the front step. It was one thing to leave something out of a story, it was another to lie.

Moses continued. "Every time the man come, he sit in the car. He wait for the men. How did they catch the man?" She looked up at Ida who dropped down on the grass next to her. Lord, give Moses strength to hear this and help me say it right.

"Moses…" When she hesitated, a look of concern came over the child's face.

"The police get the man?"

Ida tried again. "Moses, the man ran away…" An intake of breath as Moses scrambled to her feet.

"The man, he is gone?" her breathing had become shallow and fast, her eye's wide.

Ida reached up to grab Moses' arm. "He ran away without his car so the police will find him."

Moses began to shake. Her chin trembled. Ida pulled the child down to her and held her tight. "The police are doing everything they can to find him. You and I will ask God to help them?"

Moses' trembling grew more agitated. "He can come here. He can find us."

"No. No. He is running away from us. He knows if he comes here, the police will get him and he will be sent to prison."

Moses began to rock as she'd done when Ida first met her. Ida's arms grew tighter. "Moses, you are no longer alone. You have a *mama* to take care of you. I love you and I will never let anything bad like that happen to you again." Even as she said it, Ida knew it was a promise only God could help her keep.

*

As the week passed, some of the tension in Moses eased. Each day, Ida contacted Jawena to ask for an update on Dube. Each time it was the same: "Sorry, Mrs. Morgan. No news yet."

This changed on Friday. The phone rang. Ida picked it up and said, "Hello?" She pressed the phone to her ear. Sitting on the sofa opposite her, Shelly Link leaned forward, listening to her speak on the phone. "May I speak to Sergeant Jawena, please?" Ida waited. "Okay, could you ask him to phone me, please? It's Ida Morgan." She put down the phone and started for the kitchen to put on the kettle. The phone rang. She rushed back to pick it up. "Sergeant Jawena? Thanks for getting back to me so soon." She lowered herself onto a chair. "I was just wondering if you'd heard any more about Officer Dube?"

She nodded every now and then. She put down the phone. "At last. They think he's traveling on foot to Mozambique. A policeman in Malelane saw him walking past the Engen Garage late one night. He recognized Dube from the days he used to work in White River. Dube looked a bit scruffy but the policeman felt sure it was him. When he called to him, Dube fled. The policeman gave chase but lost him. They think he's living off strangers or stealing food, because his wife has his credit card."

Shelly stared at Ida, who was looking thoughtful. "Something else is eating you, Ida."

"I guess I can't get the other man out of my mind."

"The guy who murdered Tony?"

"Hmm."

Shelly waited for her to continue.

"I hate him." Ida stood up and glared out the front window. "He took my life away. He's been hounding me day and night for two years. Even when I close my eyes, he stands in front of me and gloats."

"I'm so sorry, Ida."

"I dream of the day he pays for his action. But he possesses nothing worthy enough to compensate for what he's done. Not even his life."

"You want him to suffer?"

"Yes."

CHAPTER 31

The further he walked away from his home, the more Dube's optimism faded. His mouth had become dry and the pain in his stomach yelled to be filled. Like when he was young, he felt as though he was being sucked into himself because his stomach was so empty. The mangoes he picked off the tree two days ago had helped for a while, but he ate them so quickly that his stomach couldn't tolerate them, and he threw them up. Even at a rubbish dump, the dogs got there before him. He watched them tear at a rotten chicken carcass. He could smell it from where he stood.

Although he'd almost been caught at the garage, he'd given up walking at night. Hunger made you careless. Made you take risks you wouldn't normally take. And it was different now. He wasn't a child any more. Adults shouted at him, "You smell!" After all these years, he heard again the words 'Go away.' Even children threw stones at him.

He tried to wash himself and his clothes whenever he reached a stream, but there was only so much you could do to keep clean. People didn't open their doors to someone who looked like he did.

On one hand, the unruly growth of his hair and beard was a good thing–it made him less recognizable. But it added to his unkempt appearance, which in turn caused stares and unkind remarks. So, darkness became his friend. At night he searched for thick bushes to sleep under. Why was this summer so much colder at night than usual? He needed to scoop out the sand to make his resting place more comfortable and warm so his bones wouldn't hurt so much.

Lying in a different furrow each night, he allowed his thoughts to escape from the cupboard in his mind and visions of his son would materialize before him.

"Where are you, *Baba*?"

In desperation he would try to reach out to the boy, but his arms and legs were unyielding tree trunks weighted to the floor while his voice locked in his throat. He could never reach his son. The child would fade into emptiness as he slowly returned to consciousness.

Then, sometimes, truth leached into his memories and he knew that the boy he loved would never know it. How do you give what you've never been given or show what you've never learned?

Now the ache in his heart was greater than the ache in his

stomach. And it was too late. Too much. The pain—unbearable.

He closed his eyes. He would find a way to end it. Tomorrow. Emptiness swallowed him and he knew no more until he felt the warmth of the sun on his face and a gentle tapping on his shoulder the next morning. He shrank back against the far edge of his furrow, into the bush behind him.

Squatting just a foot away from him, a toddler with her hands resting in the threadbare skirt stretched across her knees watched him. In her hand she grasped a half-eaten apple. She extended it to him.

Her sweet innocence reflected back to him a mirror to his soul. There was no way to hide the filth and corruption that lay there. Hate? He could defend himself against it. Unkindness? He could fight. Pain? He could stuff it. But love? There was no protection against it. He lay in the dirt, exposed. And he wept. Bitter tears of regret. Children had brought him wealth at the cost of everything they had, except life itself. This child had brought him mercy.

And he was undone.

CHAPTER 32

By the time Rene had put Estelle to bed, Japie had disappeared into his study and closed the door. All she wanted to do was sleep. She crept passed the study door on her way to the bedroom.

"Rene, is that you?"

She sighed. "I'm going to bed."

"Come and talk to me for a minute."

She opened the door to find him sitting in one of the easy chairs facing the window.

"I've been thinking." He patted the chair next to him. "I want to add another bedroom to the end of the house."

She couldn't look at him. "Why, Japie?"

"It's time we gave Estelle a brother or sister." He turned to smile at her.

This couldn't be happening. Whatever she said, it was going to set him off again. She said nothing.

"Well, what do you think? Estelle needs someone her age to play with."

If she told the truth, it would start a massive argument. If she lied, she would be selling her soul.

"What's the matter?" She watched him heat up. "What's wrong now? Don't you want any more children?"

"I do, but not under the present circumstances."

"What are you talking about, Rene?"

"We're not happy–you and I. How can we bring a child into the world when we don't get on?" She'd finally said it.

"We get on just fine. I can't believe you're still harping on about what happened with Edward. You need to let it go."

"Japie. I can't get beyond your inability to apologize to Edward and thank him for saving Estelle's life."

"I will not apologize. I did what I thought was best for Estelle. It's my job to protect the family. Anyway he should have told me straight away what had happened. If he hadn't..."

Rene pushed herself out of the seat.

"Sit down." His voice grew harsh. "We're having a discussion." He jumped up.

Rene felt her body become tense as her anxiety rose. She braced herself for what she was about to say. "I cannot live with this between us. You have a principle of not saying sorry and I can no longer live with it. It's one thing not to apologize to me, but Edward saved Estelle's life." She moved toward the door but Japie beat her to it and blocked the doorway.

"Please let me through." She folded her arms and stared at the floor. He glared at her, his arms stretched stiffly at his side. "Please." She wasn't giving in this time. He remained silent and still.

"Japie, I need to go to bed."

"Not till you sort this out." His voice was calm again.

"Tell you what, Japie. If you do the right thing with Edward, I will enter into a discussion with you about our future together but not until then."

Finally, and for the first time during an argument in their ten-year marriage, he moved aside. She went to bed.

CHAPTER 33

Simeon sat on a brick wall outside the hospital gates and waited for his grandmother to arrive. "You should stay here until you're feeling stronger," the doctor had said. But he wanted to get home. By the time he'd reached the wall where he now sat, he regretted his decision but the thought of walking all the way back up the hill to the hospital was more than he could bear.

Each time a taxi-bus stopped nearby, he searched for the rounded figure of his *Gogo*. After an hour of waiting, he was beginning to feel lightheaded. He shifted his position on the wall again, wedged the end of one of his crutches into a crack in the sidewalk and rested his bandaged head against it. Closing his eyes, he felt some relief from the glare of the sun. That was better.

Gradually, his mind drifted toward sleep and his body sagged against the crutches. In the background he heard approaching footsteps and the murmur of voices. Then, *thwack!* His head dropped violently forward as the crutch slipped from under his head. An explosion of pain. The sensation of falling... tumbling to the ground.

Then, laughter.

Familiar laughter. He strained to see who had kicked the crutch from under him.

The boys from the cemetery.

Tears stung his eyes as he watched them amble off. Friends shoving each other in carefree banter. If they recognized him, they didn't show it.

A pair of strong arms gripped Simeon under the arms. "Sorry. Sorry," the man said.

Simeon looked up into the face of the security guard at the hospital gate.

"I know those boys," the man said. "One day they will end up in prison." He hauled Simeon onto his feet. Simeon cried out.

"I think you should be in hospital." The man saw Simeon's tight face. "I can ask someone to help you go back."

Simeon shook his head. "I am here because those boys put me in the hospital. I do not want to stay here."

"Did you tell the police?" The security guard poked around in his pant pockets, withdrawing an old receipt and a pen.

"No."

"What is your name and where do you live?" When he'd written the details on the back of the receipt, he walked away, shaking his head.

Simeon thought no more about it. He knew he didn't have the strength to pull himself back onto the wall. So, using the crutches to brace himself against the wall, he propped himself up as best he could. It was only as he raised his head that he noticed the people standing around staring. Where are you, *Gogo*?

Finally, there she was. Alighting from a taxi-bus across the street, she hurried over. "I saw what happened." She tried to put her arms around him.

"*Gogo*, please do not touch me. I am very sore."

His grandmother waved to a taxi arriving from the opposite direction and yelled, "Wait for us!" Then, with the help of a kind stranger on one side and his *Gogo* on the other, Simeon shuffled to the taxi and headed home.

Simeon and *Gogo* were the last to be dropped off. The driver stopped next to the Daylight Hair 'Saloon' and waited. Simeon stared absently at the misspelled word on the sign, painted in uneven writing on the wall, and wondered how he was going to walk the last kilometer home. He leaned forward to speak to the driver. "*Numzane*, Sir. I have come from the hospital. Will you take me closer to my home?"

The driver pondered a few moments. "It will be R9. Each."

Gogo searched her handbag. "I have R8. Please will you still take the boy? I will walk."

He shrugged. "I will take you too, *Gogo*." The driver slid the van into first and turned into the track that led to their home. When the road became too bad, the driver stopped. "You will get out here." He refused the R8 and a grateful Simeon started his painful walk to the end of the track.

It was all so wonderfully familiar. There was *Gogo*'s rickety wooden spaza shop next to her house, waiting for her to spread out her stock of vegetables, chips and sweets for the day. Mrs. Kudzi from across the way was heading their way. Probably coming to buy something and catch up on the news.

Simeon hobbled through the front door that *Gogo* opened for him and into the kitchen-lounge where he flopped onto an old grey sofa, rescued from the dump a long time ago.

Without a word, *Gogo* scooped a mug of cold water from a bucket on the floor and handed it to Simeon. "I must go sell at my spaza shop." She headed for a corner of the kitchen where she hefted a large box of vegetables onto her turban-wrapped head and shuffled out the door. Simeon watched her. At 74, years of grinding physical work had left her stooped and slow. She dropped the box into a squeaky wheelbarrow and returned to the house for more stock. When the wheelbarrow was full, she plodded off for the spaza at the end of the garden.

Simeon reached over the side of the sofa and pulled a plastic bag onto his lap. He untied the knot that kept the goggas out and withdrew a thick pile of newspaper cuttings tucked into the pages of an A4-sized exercise book and a pen. The cuttings he placed next to him on the sofa, and then he opened the book. On the first page were three clear, neat plans for a five-roomed house.

The largest bedroom had '*Gogo*' written inside it in red writing. Next to each door he'd drawn a star to indicate the light switch. When his dream became reality, *Gogo* would never again have to light a candle to see what she was doing at night. A wash-basin had been drawn in pencil, next to the window, with two tiny taps carefully sketched in. No more trips to the communal tap.

Next, he picked up the cuttings; once more he studied the pictures of the beds he'd cut out of the advertisement section. It needed to be a soft bed that took away the pains she tried to hide each morning. His *Gogo* was going to smile again.

He lowered the book and stared out the doorway opening his view to the street. So many young people out there had set out, confident they would find a job after finishing school. He watched them. One by one they returned and told him, "You'll never get a job." Each time, he steeled his heart and told himself that he was different. Miracles happened to those who worked hard. Anyway, Mrs. Morgan believed in him, and he was also beginning to believe in himself.

First he'd get a job. Then he'd build the house. Then… He turned to the last page in the book. A single word was written at the top. FATHER. Next to the margin, going down the page, the lines were numbered 1 to 6. Next to each number, a question.

1. NAME? Sibelo…..?
2. ADDRESS? (blank)
3. PHONE NUMBER? (blank)
4. WORK? (blank)
5. FAMILY? (blank)
6. FRIENDS? (blank)

The only thing he knew was his father's first name. Why hadn't his mother ever talked about him? He had to find another way to ask *Gogo*. She got so mad whenever he questioned her. When he thought of his father and how they were going to be friends, feelings of wholeness stole over him and the longing grew intense. Finding Father was going to permanently fill the empty places inside.

CHAPTER 34

He had managed to slink away from the little girl without taking her apple, but Dube felt the demons of a guilty conscience swirl around him, mocking and jeering. Through the haze and confusion he had one clear thought: he must go back. He turned round and headed home. One more job to do. No; possibly two, before he ended his misery.

He walked slower now. Jerky movements jarred his bony hips and knees. His clothes no longer left his body to be washed. What was the point? People treated him like a tick. Like something to be ground under their feet. He never allowed himself to get too near anyone. He'd got used to his smell but strangers hadn't, nor were they shy about telling him.

Then, one day he neared an area that looked vaguely familiar to his tired, starving brain. He blinked and leaned against a tree, inspecting the area around him. The pastor. His pastor lived here. Was he still alive? He would be very old now. A splinter of hope entered his mind. He tried to concentrate.

It looked different. New brick houses had replaced old shacks, but that hill over there… he and Hat Man had played there. It was their castle. They fought and won many battles on it. If he walked to the tree that now towered over the small hill, it would remind him of the direction of the pastor's house.

A few more steps and he would see. He turned his aching body around, and there between two giant fever trees, was the pastor's house. Or, rather, what was left of it. Hope trickled out. No one could live in that place. But, perhaps he could spend the night there without being harassed.

The door had long since fallen off its hinges; it was probably used for firewood. He stepped through the crumbling doorway. Someone must be living here. The mix of ash and half burnt wood in the middle of the room said the fire was recently made. Even as he stood there, the sun's light was disappearing off the horizon. His eyes grew accustomed to the dark interior. In the far corner he made out the huddled figure of a woman curled up on a flattened cardboard box, asleep.

He leaned against the wall. He knew the woman might fight him for her space. If he kept quiet and lay in the opposite corner he may get away with a peaceful night's sleep. He tiptoed over to the corner, pulled the debris away from his spot, and lay down.

He didn't know another thing until a soft voice at the doorway the next morning said, "*Sawubona, numzane.* Did you sleep well?" He opened his eyes. The figure silhouetted in the doorway reminded Dube of a vulture. Small bent back, long scraggy neck, with a head tottering on top. Could it be?

"Pastor?" He shot up from his position and took a step in the old man's direction.

"Yes? I am Pastor Longwe. Who are you?"

Dube opened his mouth to speak, but nothing came out—only shuddering sobs bubbling up from somewhere in his stomach. He crumpled slowly to the floor, his head falling into his hands.

Pastor Longwe shuffled over to him. "What is wrong? Who are you?"

"I am Samuel Dube. Do you remember me?"

"Samuel? Of course I remember you." He lifted the bushy face to see him better. "I heard you became a policeman. I knew you would do well. You were clever and you had a fire inside you. But something has happened to you." He reached out gnarled fingers to the visitor, "Come. We can talk. My house is next door."

Sitting on a plastic chair outside the pastor's house, Dube dumped his truck load of garbage at the pastor's feet: all the sadness of a life never fully lived. Broken dreams. Broken promises. He told him everything. At first Pastor Longwe said nothing, but when Dube came to the part about taking the men to the children, the old man clutched his chest and spoke so softly that Dube had trouble hearing him.

"You said you will never do to children what was done to you." Dube saw the pain in his eyes. "You know how it feels. Why?"

For several minutes Dube couldn't speak. He shrugged and the movement echoed through his hollow soul. "I do not know. My heart is a rock. I cannot feel for myself. I cannot feel for the children."

The pastor began to shake. "Little children. Little children. You who are loved by the Father." He lifted his head to Heaven and cried. "Oh, my Father, help them."

Dube rose without a sound. His gaze fixed on the old man–the only adult who had ever shown him love. He watched the wrinkled eyes squeezed shut, the shrunken body sway on his chair. He heard the voice. "So much suffering." Tears traveled down deep tracks in the weathered face.

Dube backed away, his tread silent on the grey sand. When he reached the path he turned with bowed head and hobbled toward home. The only thing he really wanted to tell the old man never left his lips.

"Samuel." The voice behind him was stronger now, but Samuel Dube never stopped walking. "It's never too late," the old man shouted after him. "God still loves you."

CHAPTER 35

Ida lay in bed a week later, listening to the burble and splash of rain as it tumbled out the drainpipe. In the dimness of early dawn, she sank back against her pillows. So peaceful. Tea would be good. She closed her eyes. No more empty days and lonely nights. 'Me' time was rare these days, but she'd never go back. Finding homes for the other six children was also looking very positive. All good.

"*Mama?*" Two sleepy brown eyes popped around the door to her bedroom and stared seriously at her. She smiled, "Come." She stretched out her arms to Surprise. He grabbed the bedspread and twisted himself round to haul himself onto the bed. She watched her little guy. "Pull hard." She reached out a hand to help him. He dragged himself up and crawled over to her and tucked himself into bed next to her.

The phone rang. She sighed and picked it up.

"Hello, Mrs. Morgan…Mrs. Morgan?"

"Simeon? Is that you?"

"*Yebo.*" She heard the smile in his voice.

"Simeon, I'll phone you back then you can tell me what happened." His pay-as-you-go telephone card would run out long before they could share their stories.

He picked up on the first ring.

"Where are you, Simeon? What happened?"

"Some boys beat me and I was in the hospital." Typical. Just the facts. "But I am okay now."

"Tell me what happened." For the next few minutes Ida listened quietly, but by the time he reached the part of the incident at the hospital, she was overheating. "I'm so sorry, Simeon." She struggled to speak. "I don't know why they would do such a terrible thing to you. I'm so sorry."

"It is okay, Mrs. Morgan. I am getting better now."

"Why doesn't someone do something about those boys?"

"Mrs. Morgan. The boys have no one to tell them how to live. Most of them have no father and they do not listen to their mama or *gogo.*"

Out of the mouths…

"What about you? Where are you now?"

"I am at home. *Gogo* is looking after me."

168

"I'm very glad."

There was a pause.

"Mrs. Morgan, will you help me?"

"Of course. What do you need?"

"I heard today the boys who beat me are at the police station. The police want to talk to me."

Ida felt her heart constrict. "Why, Simeon?"

"The police want me to make a statement. About the boys hurt me. I need bus money to go to the police station. Mrs. Morgan, I will pay you back when I am better."

"But did you report the attack?"

"No, they catch the boys steal a woman's handbag outside the hospital. The security guard tell the police about me."

"Will you see the boys?"

"I want to."

"I don't think it's a good idea. They've damaged your body and if you see them," she placed her hand over her heart, "they may hurt you inside, too."

But Simeon insisted. When Ida realized the boy was determined she said, "Okay, Simeon. I'll take you."

"It is okay, Mrs. Morgan. I can go by myself."

"I want to go with you. It sounds like you still need help. I'll come and get you this afternoon."

After Ida wrote down the detailed description of how to get to Simeon's house, they agreed on a time and she replaced the phone. She'd ask Shell to watch the kids.

That whole morning, Ida's thoughts kept returning to the possible outcome of their visit to see the boys and it filled her with deep uneasiness. What if the charges didn't stick and they went after Simeon? She couldn't keep him safe. At least if she was with him at the police station, maybe the boys would know he had some support and leave him alone.

At three o'clock she set off. Navigating the tracks to Simeon's house went reasonably well until she had to turn left at the green *jo-jo*. It wasn't long before she ended up in a dead end and realized she must have turned left at the wrong green plastic water tank. She jumped out of the car to look for the best way to get turned round. In the grass on the lower edge of the track lay spiky remnants of broken bottles. On the upper edge, the rain had eroded deep furrows in the track. She had to reverse and reversing was top of her list of least enjoyable activities.

She glanced at her watch. She had some catching up to do. She closed her eyes, breathed in deeply, and set off slowly, the car engine shouting in protest. Five minutes later she was turned around but nothing seemed familiar. Had she gone too far? The first stirrings of panic. Where was she?

She should ask someone. Two houses down, two women sat outside a house, chatting loudly to each other.

"Excuse me," Ida said as she approached them. "*Sanibonani*. I am lost. Can you tell me where there is a *jo-jo* near here?" The women looked blankly at her. "Do you understand siSwati? English?" she asked. They stared back.

She returned to her car. The stirrings bubbled to the surface. Get a grip. Start again. Close your eyes. Breathe slowly. Now, look around you. Do you see anything familiar? She decided to go back the way she'd just come from and see if anything registered.

Over there! That untidy field of maize. Yes, she'd passed it the first time round. Hallelujah. This time she made a left instead of a right, and there was the *jo-jo* and Simeon sitting on the step in front of his tiny brick home. A few steps away, his *gogo* hung wet washing on the wire fence.

Ida climbed out, smiling the smile of the deeply thankful.

She greeted *Gogo,* who showed a perfect row of white teeth in response, then she and Simeon left for the police station.

When they entered the police station, Ida helped Simeon squeeze into a row of people sitting on a bench. She tucked an old shoulder-bag filled with newspaper under his injured leg since it was still encased in a cast, raising it off the floor while they waited. She then went and stood in line to be attended to.

Finally, half an hour later, a man behind the counter shouted, "Simeon Phiri?" When he saw Simeon's raised hand, the man waved to him and indicated he should enter a small office leading off the reception area. Ida followed Simeon and when she reached the door, there sat Sergeant Jawena behind the desk. He rose.

"Good afternoon, Mrs. Morgan. Are you well?" Ida smiled and extended her hand to him.

"Much better than when I saw you last."

"That is good." He returned her smile. "I am thinking this is the young man you were worried about?" He faced Simeon and shook his hand.

She nodded. When all three were seated, Jawena slipped a page of single photos in front of Simeon. "I am dealing with your problem personally. Do you know any of these people?"

Simeon scanned the photos one by one. He pointed out three of the faces.

"How do you know them?"

"They are three of the boys who attacked me."

"There were more?"

"Yes, there are five altogether."

Jawena slid another page of photos over to Simeon. "Are they here anywhere?"

He searched again. "Yes, I think so." He pointed to two more faces. "This one is the leader." He tapped the first one on the page. "He is small but very strong."

Jawena opened a red file and picked up a pen. "Simeon, I need you to tell me everything that you can remember about the attack. Then I want you to tell me about the incident at the hospital."

An hour later, Jawena leaned back in his chair and held up the paper he had been working on. "Read through this. If it is all correct, please date and sign it at the bottom."

Ida raised her left hand to read her watch. Jawena noticed.

"We are almost done, Mrs. Morgan."

When Simeon handed over the signed document, Jawena said, "Two more things. First, come with me to the holding cell. Let us make double sure we have the right boys. Then I want to take photos of your injuries. I will have the hospital records sent over later today."

Ida grabbed Jawena's arm. "Does he really have to see them?"

"Mrs. Morgan." Simeon faced her with a smile. "I want to do this."

Ida sighed and followed the two of them. Jawena took them behind the counter, through a door at the back of the room, and down some steps outside to a concrete courtyard that was double the size of a netball field. Skirting the near side of the courtyard, they walked down a cement pathway that flanked a long, brick building without windows.

They passed several red doors until they came to the last one. Number 7. Jawena unlocked the heavy steel door and ushered them into a tiny waiting area at the entrance of the cell. Weighty metal bars that were ten feet tall separated the waiting area from the cell. A cell within a cell.

On the other side of the bars, five young men sat against the wall of their twenty by twenty enclosure. Ida noticed the twenty foot 'ceiling' above them; open to the elements except for a giant grill of reinforced steel. The sun was past its highest, and beat through the grill down on the opposite side of the cell to where the youths sat. They stopped talking when their visitors arrived and turned to face them. One by one, they stood and disappeared through an opening at the back of the cell where the covered sleeping area must have been.

"You come back here or I'll come and get you." Jawena did not shout. He waited. "One!... Two!... Three!..." On three, all five appeared in the opening.

"Come here and stand in a line in front of me."

The shortest youth leaned against the wall and watched his friends move forward. Jawena smacked the bars with his truncheon and the youth sauntered to join the others.

Jawena turned to Simeon and said quietly. "Do you recognize any of these boys?"

Simeon looked and searched each face. "They are the ones who beat me." He faced the shortest one with an unblinking gaze. "This is the leader."

"Moswa?"

He nodded.

Moswa leaned forward and spat at Simeon. He began to laugh.

Simeon watched as the spittle ran down the bars in front of him.

"You are a coward," Moswa continued but Ida noticed his hands begin to shake. "You are weak."

"Maybe," Simeon said, "but I am free."

Moswa rushed at the bars. Simeon and Ida stepped back while Jawena raised his stick. Simeon grabbed hold of Jawena's arm. "Don't hurt him," his voice urgent. "I would be like him but my *Gogo* saved my life. This boy can beat my body but he cannot beat my soul unless I say he can." Once more he stepped forward. "I forgive you, Moswa. One day when you are tired of fighting the world, remember God. He wants to forgive you. He loves you."

Ida couldn't stand any more. She grabbed Simeon's arm and propelled him out of the cell into the sunshine.

"What are you doing?" She gripped his shoulders, longing to shake him. "He deserves to be punished."

"Yes, Mrs. Morgan. He will be, but you cannot put out fire with fire. There is a fire burning inside him that will never go out unless someone pours water on it. Love puts out fires. Not anger or hate. Sergeant Jawena has his job to do and I must do mine."

The heat in Ida's face was no longer anger but dented pride. "I'll think about it," she said, but she already knew there was truth in what he said. She heard the key turn in the lock behind them.

"May we go now?" she asked Jawena, then hung her head in embarrassment. "I'm sorry. Thank you for helping Simeon today. I really appreciate it."

"We will take photos, then you may go."

CHAPTER 36

"Mrs. Morgan? It's Sergeant Jawena." He sounded good over the phone.

"Are you phoning me to tell me good news?"

"You could say that," he said. "Just a minute." Ida could hear him speaking to someone on the other end of the line. He returned to the phone. "Sorry about that. Mrs. Morgan, we are close to getting Sergeant Dube."

Ida let out a shriek.

"We have had a sighting."

"Here in South Africa? In Mozambique? Where?"

"Closer to home. Near White River."

"But I thought you said…" Ida was beginning to feel porcupine quills. "What's he doing coming back here?" Her conversation with Moses flicked into her mind.

"We do not know yet. An off-duty policeman chased a man when he tried to steal food from a woman's spaza shop next to the main road."

"What makes you think it's him?"

"Well, the policeman said the man's hair was wild but he noticed a small area of white hair near his right eyebrow. He…"

"I remember." Ida said. "Sergeant, you don't think he wants to harm the children, do you?"

"I do not know why he is coming back. It does not make sense. If he is caught he will go to jail for a long time."

"What if the man wants revenge? What if he puts two and two together and knows I was involved?" Ida felt the pressure of her old enemy, fear, take control. "I was the one who reported the children."

"Mrs. Morgan, we are doing what we can to find him. Keep the usual precautions. Lock your doors. Watch the children. You will be fine."

Ida slowly put down the phone. Yeah, right. Watch the children. Watch your back. Why was this happening now, just as her life was getting back on track? When was it all going to stop?

She walked across the kitchen to close the window a little. She looked outside and noticed workmen next door at the Van Reenens. Were they building onto their house?

CHAPTER 37

He was almost home. After the scare at the spaza shop, Dube had almost given up, but something happened to spur him on. As he ran from the shop, followed closely by a man, some children ran into the road to see what all the fuss was about and collided with his pursuer. By the time the man untangled himself, Dube was long gone. His first bit of luck in a long time.

But he knew his time was running out. Lack of food and diarrhea, probably from bad drinking water, had sapped strength from his already weakened body. He now concentrated on putting one foot in front of the other. Head down, he stared at his feet. Left. Right. Left. Right. One kilometer. Two.

He raised his head. His heart began to pound. Not long now. The last hill before home. The sun told him it was midday. His son was still at school. He'd wait under some trees until the heat lessened. Then he'd take a parallel path up the hill just in case neighbors spotted him. He wanted to be there to greet his son ahead of his wife.

Someone had left a plastic water-bottle half-filled with water next to an abandoned mini-market at the base of the hill. He swiveled around. No one seemed to be watching. He sucked it down with one gulp and threw the bottle to the earth. Now for some shade.

How many times had he driven up this track? He knew every pothole, every twist in the road, every house built alongside it. He followed the road in his mind. There was a cluster of trees a short way up the hill on the left. Just what he needed. He made it there without anyone paying any attention to him. That thick bush over there would be just fine to rest under. But when he reached it, he noticed the bush grew in rocky soil. Stones were not made for comfort. He decided to move further up the hill.

Being so close to home lifted his spirits. There were things that needed to be said to his son, Benson. He felt he could say them now. He had nothing else to lose. He would tell him things he'd always been too busy to say while he was working.

After he'd spoken to his son, he had one more stop. Mrs. Morgan. He knew it was her. It had to be. This time alone on the road had given him time to work it all out. He remembered Jawena speaking to her on the phone one day. He didn't think much of it at the time. What was it Jawena had said? Something about 'Did the kids have the facts right?' Then he had said, 'If we are going to help them we must be sure.' It had sounded unimportant at the time but now it all made sense. It had to be her.

After he had visited Morgan, he didn't care what happened.

His mouth began to water thinking of the food Benson would bring him. His son would get him some clean clothes and his razor. Maybe he would even make some excuse to get his mother out of the house so his father could have a proper wash.

He needed to travel further up the hill. He had a thought. Of course! What about the banana trees in his own garden? They were at the back of the property. He could hide there. Not even Mrs. Ncube had eyes that could see through them. He would hear Benson as soon as he turned up.

He stepped onto the soil of his home and felt an odd mixture of belonging and despair. He was home, but not for long. He would enjoy it while it lasted. The cool, clean earth around the bananas reminded him his wife had one redeeming feature: she kept a clean house. He lay down, twisting this way and that to find a comfortable position to have a snooze. In the end, he lay on his back, closed his eyes, and waited for his son.

A familiar voice shocked him into wakefulness. She'd come home yelling and he hadn't heard her arrive. He could have kicked himself. He'd missed his opportunity to speak to Benson alone. So she was picking on Benson now, was she? She didn't have a husband to yell at. Well, maybe he should do something about that, too, before he left. He sat and listened.

He heard the shouting as it moved to the kitchen but he couldn't understand the words. Dube edged to the end of the banana trees and stuck his head around the corner to see better. Through the kitchen window he could see Benson retreat to the far side of the kitchen. Into view came her arms, beating the air. Then the rest of her followed, her arm wings vibrating with exertion. Nothing had changed. Only, this time, Dube was no longer the focus of her attention. It was all too much. Benson did not deserve this.

Thunder suddenly rumbled across the darkening sky. His head shot up. The clouds were at bursting point, ready to drop their load.

He shouted, "Woman, come outside!" This was not part of his plan, but this was his moment.

The yelling stopped. Two faces appeared at the window. The woman whispered to Benson, then disappeared for a moment, reappearing when the door flew open. The faces of Benson's cousins joined him at the window. They watched the woman leave the house.

"Who is it? Is it you, monkey man?" She stomped down the steps, throwing her body from side to side with each step she took.

A blinding flash of lightning illuminated Dube's position–just in front of the bananas. She took a step back when she saw him. "*Eeish.* What happened to you?" She thrust a pudgy finger in his direction. "Go back to the dump where you belong. Do not let Benson see you like this."

The clouds emptied their burden.

Dube took a step toward her. His eyes narrowed as the stinging rain slashed at him from the side. "My son is a good boy." His voice carried forth with surprising power through the pounding volley of rain. "You will not hurt him again." He lunged forward to grab her. His foot slipped on the quickly forming mud. He thudded face-down into the sludge. He wiped the worst of the mud away from his eyes and saw her look of terror. She turned back to escape into the house. Her foot twisted under her, and her head came down with an almighty thud on the edge of the bottom step.

The last thought of Samuel Dube was that the count of orphans had just gone up by three.

CHAPTER 38

Ida couldn't sleep. The scene at the police station with Simeon whirled around her head, interrupting every attempt to fall asleep. At three a.m. she finally stopped justifying her need for revenge and began to search for the truth. She, who had so much in life, gave so little, while Simeon who had so little, gave love. She knew if she was going to move on, she had to choose.

But then again, forgiving someone who'd stolen your car was easy. This was murder... How quickly her thoughts jumped back into the sludge of her thoughts. Why was this so hard?

She dragged her mind back. Revenge or freedom. Those were her options. Why couldn't she have both? But, if she was honest, she knew that revenge was like a mouse to a hungry lion; it only awakened a desire for real meat. And the real meat of revenge, wasn't just about justice, it was about inflicting pain and suffering on the perpetrator. Simeon was so free from all that. He had no one shackled to his leg that he lugged around like she did.

More than anything, she wanted to be free from this. Simeon had shown her that, just as her mother had said, it wasn't a war to be won it was a choice to be made. She made her decision. She chose to forgive. "When I'm tempted to take it back, Lord, please help me."

She closed her eyes. Finally she slept.

The next morning, Ida woke before dawn to the clear song of the heuglin's robin outside her window. She opened her eyes, heavy in sleep, and thrust a pillow over her head. Too early! But the robin insisted on its role as community alarm clock. She gave up. Throwing the blanket aside, she padded to the kitchen and switched on the kettle. From behind the closed curtains came the soft drumming of rain against the window.

The phone rang. "Did I wake you up? It's Sergeant Jawena."

"No, the birds did. What can I do for you?"

"Mrs. Morgan, the hunt is over. Officer Dube has been found."

"Thank God. He's in custody?" Ida stood up and drew back the curtains.

"Actually, he's dead. Both he and his wife were found dead outside his house."

Ida sunk down onto her kitchen chair. "What happened?"

"We're not sure. There will be an autopsy to see how they died.

Apparently, his son says both his parents slipped and fell. Investigators think he was weakened by lack of food and disease and lying in the rain too long."

He waited. "Mrs. Morgan, you must be happy?"

She thought for a moment. "Not happy. Relieved. It's a funny thing, Sergeant. I feel like I've been waiting for a tornado to land on me but it's just passed me by. Now I can get on with my life." She thanked him and put down the phone.

With her tea in her hand, Ida wandered over to what was now the children's room. On the floor lay two temporary foam mattresses—both unoccupied. On the single bed lay Moses, her brothers sprawled on either side of her. Ida gazed at her children, then bent down and gently kissed each warm forehead. She tiptoed to the window and, careful not to wake them, pulled aside the curtain. On the horizon, the clouds parted and she felt the warmth of the sunshine on her face. She closed her eyes and whispered, "Thank you."

CPSIA information can be obtained at www.ICGtesting.com
Printed in the USA
LVOW080838270712

291756LV00005B/2/P